A Frank M... Crime Thriller #3

SIMON MCCLEAVE

STAMFORD
PUBLISHING

DEADLY CARE

by Simon McCleave

A Marshal of Snowdonia Murder Mystery

Frank Marshal Crime Thriller
Book 3

No part of this publication may be reproduced, stored, or transmitted in any form or by any means, electronic, mechanical, photocopying, recording, scanning, or otherwise without written permission from the publisher. It is illegal to copy this book, post it to a website, or distribute it by any other means without permission.

Names, characters, businesses, places, events, and incidents are either the products of the author's imagination or used in a purely fictitious manner. Any resemblance to actual persons, living or dead, or actual events is purely coincidental.

First published by Stamford Publishing Ltd in 2025

Copyright © Simon McCleave, 2025
All rights reserved

❦ Created with Vellum

BOOKS BY SIMON McCLEAVE

THE DI RUTH HUNTER SERIES

#1. The Snowdonia Killings
#2. The Harlech Beach Killings
#3. The Dee Valley Killings
#4. The Devil's Cliff Killings
#5. The Berwyn River Killings
#6. The White Forest Killings
#7. The Solace Farm Killings
#8. The Menai Bridge Killings
#9. The Conway Harbour Killings
#10. The River Seine Killings
#11. The Lake Vyrnwy Killings
#12. The Chirk Castle Killings
#13. The Portmeirion Killings
#14. The Llandudno Pier Killings
#15. The Denbigh Asylum Killings
#16. The Wrexham Killings
#17. The Colwyn Bay Killings
#18. The Chester Killings
#19. The Llangollen Killings
#20. The Wirral Killings
#21. The Abersoch Killings

THE DC RUTH HUNTER MURDER CASE SERIES

#1. Diary of a War Crime
#2. The Razor Gang Murder
#3. An Imitation of Darkness
#4. This is London, SE15

THE ANGLESEY SERIES - DI LAURA HART

#1. The Dark Tide
#2. In Too Deep
#3. Blood on the Shore
#4. The Drowning Isle
#5. Dead in the Water

PSYCHOLOGICAL THRILLERS

Last Night at Villa Lucia
Five Days in Provence

About the Author

Simon McCleave is a multi million-selling crime novelist who lives in North Wales with his wife and two children.

Before he was an author, Simon worked as a script editor at the BBC and a producer at Channel 4 before working as a story analyst in Los Angeles. He then became a script writer, writing on series such as *Silent Witness*, *The Bill*, *EastEnders* and many more. His Channel 4 film *Out of the Game* was critically acclaimed and described as '*an unflinching portrayal of male friendship*' by *Time Out*.

His first book, *'The Snowdonia Killings'*, was released in January 2020 and soon became an Amazon Bestseller, reaching No 1 in the UK Chart and selling over 400,000 copies. His twenty subsequent novels in the DI Ruth Hunter Snowdonia Series have all been Amazon bestsellers, with most of them hitting the top of the digital charts. He has sold over 3 million books to date.

'The Dark Tide', Simon's first book in an Anglesey based crime series for publishing giant Harper Collins (Avon), was a major hit in 2022, becoming the highest selling Waterstone's Welsh Book of the Month ever.

This year, Simon is releasing a new series of books featuring Frank Marshal a retired detective who lives in Snowdonia.

Simon has also written a one-off psychological thriller, *Last Night at Villa Lucia*, for Storm Publishing, which was a major hit, *The Times* describing it as '*...well above the usual seasonal villa thriller...*' with its '*...empathetic portrayal of lives spent in the shadow of coercion and abuse.*'

The Snowdonia based DI Ruth Hunter books are now set to be filmed as a major new television series, with shooting to begin in North Wales in 2025.

Your FREE book is waiting for you now!

Get your FREE copy of the prequel to
the DI Ruth Hunter Series NOW
http://www.simonmccleave.com/vip-email-club
and join my VIP Email Club

Prologue

Monday 12th August, 2002

BRONWEN'S EYES darted around the interview room at St Asaph Police Station. She felt sick with fear. Two male detectives sat down opposite her and then brusquely placed folders and paperwork down on the table. Sitting to her right was Jessica Wright, the elderly manager of the children's home in Dolgellau where Bronwen had lived for the past two years. She had just turned thirteen. Unlike most of the kids there, she loved the home. It was much safer and more peaceful than the home she'd been brought up in; a violent, abusive chaotic mix of addiction and petty crime.

Detective Sergeant Barry Jenkins sat forward at the table and looked at her. He was overweight and his white shirt stretched at the buttons. His neck was thick, and his face red and sweaty. Next to him was Detective Constable Tim Rathbone who was in his 20s, with blond hair and a youthful face with a pointy nose.

Bronwen glanced behind her at the Duty Solicitor, Kevin Price, who had explained to her that if there were any questions that she didn't feel confident about answering, she could say 'no comment'.

Jenkins leaned over and pressed the red button on the recording machine. There was a loud electronic noise that startled her a little.

'Interview with Bronwen Thompson. Interview Room 2, St Asaph Police Station, Monday 12th August, 5.34pm. Present in this room are DC Rathbone, Duty Solicitor Kevin Price, Bronwen's appropriate adult Jessica Wright, and myself, DS Jenkins.'

Rathbone sniffed as he pulled his chair closer to the table and then looked over at her.

Bronwen's stomach was clenched tight and her palms were sweaty. She'd been arrested outside Llanfair slate mines three hours earlier. Located near Blaenau Ffestiniog, the mines were a disused labyrinth of caverns, underground paths, and pit shafts. Bronwen loved it there. She thought it was 'dead spooky'. But now everything had gone horribly wrong.

Since being arrested, she'd been handcuffed and taken to the police station where she'd been searched, fingerprinted, and photographed. Her head was whirling and it felt as if she was in some terrible dream that she was soon going to wake up from.

'Bronwen,' Rathbone said in a calm voice. 'Can you tell us where you were today?'

'I was at the slate mines,' she replied, feeling her voice tremble with nerves.

Rathbone looked at his notebook. 'That's the Llanfair slate mines, is that right?'

She nodded and took a breath to try to steady herself. She'd never been in a police station before.

'Yes,' she replied in a virtual whisper.

'What were you doing there, Bronwen?' he asked.

'I'd gone with a friend to have a look around.'

Jenkins looked directly at her with a suspicious expression.

Oh God, does he know that I'm lying to him? It felt as if he could see right through her. That he could see her lies.

'And that's Louise Dyer, is that correct?' Rathbone said.

She nodded and looked down at the floor.

'For the purposes of the tape,' Jenkins said, 'Bronwen has nodded to confirm that.'

'When officers found you,' Rathbone continued, 'you said that you didn't see what had happened to Callum Jones.'

'Yes ... I mean no, I didn't.'

Rathbone looked at her. 'You told officers that you thought Callum Jones had fallen down the pit shaft by accident?'

'Yes. I think so. I think that's what happened.'

Jenkins started to roll up the sleeves of his shirt. 'The thing is, Bronwen, that's not what your friend Louise has told us. She says that you knew Callum from school. That you'd arranged to meet him at the mines with some others because she thought Callum was going to ask you out. When Callum arrived, Louise told him that you liked him. But Callum laughed at you, said you were a skank and probably had AIDS. You then pushed him and he fell.'

'No, no ... I ...' Bronwen stammered as her eyes filled with tears. 'Why is she saying that? That's not true. He tripped and fell but his brother Stu was holding on to him.'

'Are you saying that Louise is lying?'

'Yes.'

'But you did know Callum?' Jenkins asked.

'Yes,' she sobbed.

'From school?'

'Yes.'

Jessica handed her a tissue. 'Here you go,' she whispered.

Bronwen nodded and wiped her eyes.

Jenkins frowned. 'Why would Louise make something like that up? She's your friend.'

'I don't know,' she sobbed. She had no idea why Louise had made up the story about her pushing Callum. They both knew what had happened. Why was she lying about it?

'We had a report that a group of teenagers were having a party down at the mines,' Jenkins said. 'Is that who you and Louise were with today?'

Bronwen shook her head. 'No.' She couldn't say yes, could she? She couldn't admit that she'd been so shit-faced on cheap cider that she'd puked her guts up and could hardly remember a thing about what happened earlier.

'You see, when officers arrested you they said that you smelled strongly of alcohol,' Rathbone said.

Bronwen shrugged. 'No.'

'Okay. You're telling us that despite what Louise has told us in her statement, you did not push Callum?' Rathbone asked as if this clearly wasn't true.

'No. I didn't. He just tripped up. It's dark in there,' she protested.

'And what happened after Callum tripped and fell?'

'I don't know. Everyone just ran away. I didn't see anything after that.'

Jenkins narrowed his eyes. 'Ran away?'

'I ... I don't know. Someone shouted 'police' so everyone just turned and ran.' Bronwen felt so incredibly guilty that everyone had abandoned Stu and Callum. But they were all drunk and smoking weed so no one was thinking straight. And as soon as someone mentioned the police, everyone scarpered.

Jenkins and Rathbone exchanged a look.

'Someone shouted 'police'?' Jenkins asked to clarify.

'Yes,' she whispered.

'And what was Stuart Jones doing while you were running away?' Rathbone asked.

Bronwen took a few seconds as she thought back. She was racked with guilt. 'He was holding on to his brother. Shouting for someone to help him get Callum back up. He needed someone to help him.'

Jenkins took a breath and said slowly, 'But instead, you all ran away?'

'Yes.' Bronwen gave a shameful nod as her eyes filled with tears again. Then she looked up at them. 'Is Callum all right? Is he going to be okay?'

Rathbone shook his head. 'I'm afraid Callum died from his injuries before he even got to hospital.'

Chapter 1

Monday 3rd April, 2023

ANNIE TAYLOR SAT to one side of the desk in the GP's office at Dolgellau Medical Centre. Dr Andrew Burrows sat looking at his computer screen before turning to face her.

In his mid 30s, Andrew was handsome, athletic, with intelligent blue eyes and sandy-coloured hair. He wore a pair of designer glasses which he pushed up the bridge of his nose. He had been her GP for about two years after Gerald, her doctor of over thirty years, finally decided to retire.

'So, the results from the MRI are back, Annie,' Andrew said as he turned the screen to show her. 'You've pulled these cruciate ligaments which is why there's so much inflammation, but I can also see that you've got a touch of osteoarthritis in the knee joint here. The cartilage has worn away which is why it's now stiff some of the time.'

Annie was seventy-two and her knee had been playing

up for a while. It hadn't been helped by a fall down the curb outside the butchers on Dolgellau High Street. She'd landed with all her weight on top of her right knee.

'Oh dear,' Annie replied, pulling a face. 'Osteoarthritis doesn't really go away, does it?'

Andrew took a moment then shook his head. 'Not really. And not at your age. But there are things we can do. I can prescribe you some pain relief.'

Annie shook her head. 'I'm not a big fan of pills. I don't mind the odd paracetamol or ibuprofen, but nothing stronger unless it's just short term.'

Andrew nodded. 'Okay. I'll prescribe something short term for you, and if the swelling doesn't go down, then we can inject steroids directly into your knee. You could also think about using a walking stick while it's this painful.'

A stick! Really?

Annie had a flash of herself doddering around with a walking stick and her heart sank. How had she got to the point in her life when a doctor was suggesting she used a stick? In her head, she was still in her 20s.

'Physio?' Annie enquired, ignoring his suggestion of her using a stick. It might have been vanity or pride, but she wasn't about to start hobbling around with a walking stick quite yet.

'Yes, physio is a good idea, but the waiting list is pretty long …' Andrew admitted, '… unless you can go private?'

'Yes, I can go private for that.' Annie smiled. 'All my friends seem to be getting new knees, although they are a little bit older than me.'

'We're not at that point yet, Annie,' he reassured her in his soft voice. 'I'm going to write up a prescription for some painkillers. You can pick it up on the way out.'

'Thank you.' Annie watched Andrew as he used the computer to order her prescription. If she and her late husband Stephen had ever had a son, he would have been about Andrew's age. Given the hideous events of six months ago, she was glad that they had never had children.

Andrew then turned back to face Annie. He leaned forward and gave her a meaningful look. 'And how are you generally? After everything that happened?'

After everything that happened?

She played his phrase through her head.

Sometimes she had periods of time when she forgot about those dark days. It was usually minutes, sometimes hours, but never more than that.

Six months ago, Annie's life had been turned upside down. In fact, that didn't really describe the destruction and pain that had shattered her life. It was like some terrible nightmare that, even six months on, she often thought she was going to wake up from.

To her horror, she'd discovered that Stephen had murdered her younger sister, Meg. Annie was beyond heartbroken. She and Meg had been so incredibly close. As if this wasn't enough for her to bear, it had become clear that Stephen was a serial killer who had murdered at least three women in North Wales in the late 1990s. It just made her shudder and her skin crawl. She wasn't sure it was something that she was ever going to get over. Just trying to get her head around the fact that she had shared her life, her home, and her bed with a man who had murdered innocent women made her physically sick.

Annie was still searching her memory for signs that Stephen had been a psychopath and a monster. But there was nothing. And the question that had plagued her ever since was – why? She had been unable to make sense of what he'd done, and she feared she never would. With decades as a Crown Court Judge, Annie had presided over trials of those who were so evil, perverse, and inhuman that it had chilled her to the bone. But to somehow reconcile that she'd been married to a man like that felt impossible. In addition, she was haunted by feelings of guilt - that she bore some responsibility for Stephen's murderous nature. After all, how could she not have spotted it?

'I guess it's getting easier. Very slowly,' Annie said unconvincingly. She didn't know what else to say. There were some days when that just wasn't true, and she felt that she was going backwards. And there were some days when she feared for her very sanity.

'Are you sleeping okay?' Andrew asked.

Annie shrugged. 'Sometimes. Most of the time.'

That was a lie too. There were usually vivid dreams or night terrors that made her wake in a cold sweat. She had no idea why she felt the need to placate Andrew or not tell the truth.

'We talked about medication last time, didn't we?' he asked.

She nodded. 'As I said, I'm not really a pills type of person. Maybe it's my generation.'

'Okay,' he said doubtfully, 'but if you're struggling, a short course of anti-depressants can make all the difference.'

Annie gave him a placating nod as she pushed herself to her feet and tried not to wince at the sharp pain in her knee. 'I'll bear it in mind, Andrew. Thank you.'

'Bye Annie.' Andrew returned to his computer screen and glanced at his watch. He was anxious about something.

Annie opened the door and walked gingerly down the corridor towards the reception area.

'Hi, it's Annie Taylor. Dr Burrows is printing a prescription for me,' she explained to the young receptionist who had a short fringe cut into her dark hair.

'Right, I'll just get it for you,' the receptionist said brightly as she pointed to the printer at the far side of reception.

Out of the corner of her eye, Annie spotted Andrew coming along the corridor. He was now wearing a casual navy jacket and carrying a black briefcase. Even though it was only 1.30pm, it looked like he was finishing for the day; or at least heading off somewhere else.

'Bye again,' he said under his breath as he passed her in a hurry.

'Yes, bye Andrew.' Annie took the printed prescription from the receptionist, thanked her, and then headed for the automatic double doors that led out to the car park.

The sky above was bright blue, with long thin clouds stretched out like candyfloss. The air smelled of fresh blossom and freshly cut grass. She could hear the sound of a lawnmower, and spotted someone cutting the verges of the grass banks on the far side of the car park.

Then she glanced at the disabled bays that were directly outside the door.

If my knee goes, I wonder if I can get myself a blue badge? she thought as she soldiered on. *Now that would be very useful.*

The spring sunshine was warm on Annie's face as she moved slowly across the car park to where she'd parked her Land Rover Discovery. The sun was so bright that she'd have to get her sunglasses out of the glove box. Someone had recently told her that it was no longer legal to drive in sunglasses but she was sure that couldn't be true.

Opening the passenger door, Annie leaned inside the car. She retrieved the glasses from the glove box and then walked around the front of her car to the driver's door. She looked across the car park, shielding her eyes from the sun, and spotted Andrew talking on his mobile phone as he stood beside his black Saab X9-30. He looked agitated as he spoke, but he was too far away for Annie to hear what he was talking about. And frankly, it was none of her business.

Then she saw a figure coming out from behind one of the parked cars.

At first she didn't think anything of it.

As she opened the driver's door and looked back across the car park again, she did a double take.

The figure she'd seen ten seconds earlier was wearing a black hoodie up over their head and a balaclava covering their mouth.

Oh my God. Who the hell is that? she thought anxiously.

The figure seemed to be making a deliberate beeline for Andrew.

For a second, Annie was frozen to the spot.

Her pulse quickened.

There was something very wrong about what was unfolding in front of her.

She sensed the tension deep in the pit of her stomach but she felt helpless.

Suddenly, the figure held up a handgun in a gloved hand and pointed it directly at Andrew who was still engrossed in his phone call.

'Andrew!' Annie yelled at the top of her voice, trying to warn him. 'Andrew!'

Andrew spun around to see who was shouting at him but then caught sight of the figure who had now stopped about fifteen yards away.

Oh no!

Annie's heart was thumping and her mouth dry.

CRACK!

She flinched as the air seemed to explode with the thunderous noise of the gunshot as the figure fired, the barrel flashing.

Then the figure marched towards Andrew who was now lying supine on the ground. They pointed the gun at his chest from close range and shot again.

CRACK! CRACK!

The figure then rummaged through Andrew's jacket, pulled out what looked like a wallet, and grabbed his briefcase before slowly looking around the car park.

Annie instinctively moved and ducked down behind her car out of sight.

She dropped her sunglasses which skidded along the ground and then stopped.

She winced at the searing pain in her knee as she crouched down.

Trying to get her breath, she listened carefully.

Her pulse was thundering in her ears.

What the hell is going on?

She had no idea if the figure had deliberately targeted Andrew, or if they were going to shoot indiscriminately at anyone else in the car park.

Holding her breath, she strained her hearing.

Nothing.

She pulled out her phone but hesitated calling 999.

If she spoke, she might alert the person with the gun to where she was hiding.

She listened again.

Nothing.

Then a woman screamed from somewhere.

A car engine started and revved noisily.

Poking her head above the boot of her car, Annie scanned the car park but the figure had now gone.

Andrew was lying on the ground motionless.

Oh God.

Several people were cowering behind cars over to her

right. Others were peering anxiously from behind the double doors of the medical centre.

There was a squeal of tyres as a silver VW Golf came speeding through the car park. The masked figure was behind the wheel.

Annie instinctively held her phone up and took a series of photos of the VW Golf in the hope that she'd get the licence plate.

Then her attention turned to Andrew who was not moving.

As she hobbled as fast as she could towards him, an older male GP in his 50s came sprinting across the car park, stethoscope still around his neck.

'Oh my God,' he gasped loudly as he reached Andrew.

Annie watched on in horror as the GP felt Andrew's neck for a pulse. His jacket and shirt were drenched in blood which had also pooled on the tarmac around where he was lying.

Annie was no expert, but she didn't think anyone could survive being shot three times at close range and losing that much blood.

'Andrew? Andrew?' the GP said urgently as the practice nurse arrived.

'Oh my God! What's happened?' she asked in horror.

The GP, who now had blood all over his hands and shirt sleeves, looked up at the nurse. 'Someone shot Andrew.'

The nurse grabbed her phone from her pocket. 'I'll ring for an ambulance.'

The GP gave her a dark look and shook his head.

Andrew was already dead.

Chapter 2

I pulled the reins over to the right and slowed my horse, Duke. We were in the middle of Snowdonia/Eryri National Park, approaching the rear of the graveyard at St Mary's Church in Dolgellau.

'Whoa there boy,' I said, and reached over to give him a reassuring stroke and pat of his neck.

Checking in at a mighty seventeen hands, Duke was my chestnut-coloured cob. Down to my right, Jack, my trusty German Shepherd, had stopped, his tongue hanging and his breath laboured from keeping up. But his tail wagged. He was enjoying this cross-country trek in the spring sunshine.

The field behind the church was easy going after the rough terrain that we'd covered on the way over here. Tilting my head, I looked up at the big blue sky. Even though I'd lived my whole life in this landscape, I still sometimes felt a sense of awe at the enormity of the sky above us. This was the land where I'd been born and bred. This open space where old-fashioned values are set in stone. The people of Snowdonia/Eryri were strong on principles, but also warm and compassionate about eccentric behaviour. This place was full of 'odd-bods' but they all seemed to bump along with little friction. And what often passed as modern morality seemed far less important than rock-solid common sense. Of course, there had always been a lot of teasing. People of my generation in North Wales are blunt, even ruthless, with their humour. These days they call it 'tough love', but I can see how a good dose of honesty is more useful than quiet sympathy. I don't think my wife Rachel agrees with me on that one though.

Growing up with a tough, humourless, farmer as a father taught me not to take myself too seriously. But I've made an effort not to be like him when it comes to my own children and grandchild.

Catching on to that thought, I turned back and saw that my ten-year-old grandson Sam was just behind on his beautiful white Connemara pony called Lleuad, which was Welsh for moon.

Sam was wearing a black riding helmet and a black gilet with a t-shirt underneath. I watched as he tightened his legs around the saddle and pulled on the reins to effortlessly bring the horse to a stop.

'You all right, mate?' I shouted, feeling an overwhelming sense of pride.

Sam gave me a grin and a thumbs up. 'Tidy,' he yelled back.

'Tidy?' I laughed, shaking my head. 'They only say 'tidy' down in South Wales.'

Sam looked confused. 'Do they? I saw it on the telly with Mum and Nain.'

'Come on,' I said as I took my feet out of the stirrups, threw my leg as best I could off the saddle, and dropped down to the ground. I felt a twinge across the base of my spine but that was nothing new. Everything seemed to twinge and ache a bit these days.

Sam and I walked over to the long wooden fence at the back of the church and tied up our horses. I'd shown Sam how to use a quick-release knot to secure his horse to the rail.

'Well remembered, mate,' I said encouragingly as I watched him loop the reins.

Away to our left, a pair of birds chased each other with a shrill chatter in a small cluster of sturdy oak trees. In the distance, I could hear a tractor. Probably a farmer spreading his grazing fields with fertiliser to boost spring growth so that it could be cut for hay and silage later in the year.

We climbed over the fence and then made the short walk along the pathway to go into the grounds of the church. The path was lined with beautiful clusters of bright yellow daffodils.

'I think it would be nice to take him some of these,' I suggested to Sam as I crouched down and took five daffodils from the grass. There were dozens, so I hoped that no one would mind.

'Did he like daffodils then?' Sam asked.

'Yes, he did,' I replied.

As we walked on, the wind picked up and rattled the hedges and trees that bordered the graveyard. But the wind was warm and our feet crunched on the gravel path as we cut through.

Dark green moss and lichens covered many of the older gravestones that flanked the path. The headstones were all different shapes and sizes. The lettering on them had been worn away by the wind, rain, and time itself, so that many were now illegible under their thick layers of moss.

Up ahead was a huge, towering monument of a tomb that resembled an altar, with deep indentations marking out rows of names. Its granite face was carved into grooves with seaweed-like tufts of lichen creeping outwards from the seams. Huge flowers wrapped around the base like climbing vines and extended upwards towards the sky. Battery-powered candles had been placed at its base but they had been knocked over in the wind.

Sam crouched down and put them back so they stood upright.

'Thank you, mate,' I said quietly.

The pathway reached a fork and Sam and I took the left hand path.

'How old would Uncle James have been today?' Sam asked as we approached the part of the churchyard where my parents and my son were buried.

I sighed. 'He would have been forty-two today.'

What I would have given to be celebrating his birthday with him. But James had taken his own life just over ten years ago. We didn't know why, just that he'd struggled with mental health issues all his life. He had come home a few months earlier to live with me and Rachel. And then one day, he'd taken himself off to the woods at the back of our farmhouse and hanged himself from a tree. I'd found him and carried his body home. It's not something that I or my wife Rachel would ever get over. I don't think we ever wanted to get over it or ever forget.

'Here we go, mate,' I said, pointing to James' grave.

It had taken me so long to pluck up the courage to visit. In fact, it had taken a decade. But now, every few weeks, I'd come here to lay flowers and have a little chat. When Sam had heard that it would have been James' birthday, he asked if he could come with me.

Crouching down together, Sam and I swept some

DEADLY CARE

leaves from the grave. I then took the wilted flowers that I'd left last time and popped them in a nearby bin before putting the daffodils in a small vase.

As I blinked away tears, I blew out my cheeks. Being at his grave on his birthday had really got to me.

'Happy birthday, mate,' I said, aware that my voice was a little trembly.

'Happy birthday, Uncle James,' Sam said in a virtual whisper.

I felt Sam put his hand on my shoulder reassuringly.

I gave him a smile.

Then he looked at the grave next to James' which was where my father was buried.

'Is that where your dad is buried?' he asked.

'That's right.' I nodded. 'He was your *Hen Daid*.'

Sam gave me a quizzical look.

'It's Welsh for great grandfather,' I explained. 'Actually, I think it's what we say here in North Wales. In South Wales, I think they say *Hen dad cu*.'

'What was he like?' Sam asked.

What was he like?

I thought for a few seconds. I didn't want to say that he was a hard, unemotional man prone to the odd bouts of rage and violence.

'He was a tough man,' I said.

'What did he do?'

'He was a farmer, so he worked very hard. Out in all weathers,' I replied.

Sam looked up at me. 'Did he fight in the war?'

'Yes.' I nodded. 'He enlisted as soon as he turned eighteen, and his regiment went out to fight in Burma.'

'What's Burma?'

'It's a country near Thailand, India, and China. I'm

pretty sure they changed its name to Myanmar,' I said as I searched my memory.

'Did he shoot anyone?' Sam asked quite innocently.

'I'm not sure,' I admitted. 'He didn't really ever talk about the war.'

However, mother said that he'd never been the same after he'd come back from Burma. He'd returned with malaria and suffered from horrendous nightmares. Sometimes it made me wonder if his anger and terrible moods were somehow linked to fighting the Japanese in the forests of Burma and what he'd witnessed there.

I glanced over at Sam who was deep in thought. 'Right, come on mate. Time to head back.'

'Can I come with you next time you come?' he asked.

'Of course you can.'

My phone rang.

It was Annie.

'Hi Annie,' I said as I took a step down the path.

She sounded out of breath and agitated. 'Frank?'

'Everything all right?' I asked with concern.

'No,' she replied. 'My doctor, Andrew Burrows, has just been shot dead right in front of me. I didn't know who else to call.'

'Okay, where are you?' I asked, still processing what she'd told me.

'Dolgellau Medical Centre.'

'Right. Stay there and I'll be with you in half an hour,' I reassured her.

Chapter 3

It was exactly 30 mins later by the time I drove up to the Dolgellau Medical Centre. Sam and I had galloped home and I'd left him to tether the two horses and give them some water and feed. I'd checked on my wife Rachel, who had now been suffering from Lewy Bodies Dementia for over a year. She was sitting with my daughter Caitlin in our living room which put my mind at rest. The plan had been for all of us to visit James' grave today but Rachel had become confused and agitated. Caitlin had offered to sit with her, make a cup of tea, and watch an old episode of *Inspector Morse* which always made Rachel much calmer.

The roads around central Dolgellau were chaotic with emergency vehicles and the screech of sirens. Uniformed police officers in high-vis jackets directed concerned members of the public away from the scene. There was a horribly dark and frightening atmosphere that I'd rarely witnessed in this area when I worked as a copper.

I made my way up to the small road that led into the medical centre. It was now roped off with blue and white police evidence tape. There were four uniformed officers standing by making sure that no one entered. Other officers were redirecting traffic and explaining to members of the public why the area had been cordoned off.

One of the older officers was Sergeant Johnny Wilson, who was now well into his 50s. I remembered him from when I was stationed over at St Asaph and he was a probationer.

Buzzing down the window of my Ford Ranger pick-up truck, I pulled up slowly towards where he was standing.

'I'm sorry, sir,' he said, gesticulating with his hands. 'I'm going to need you to turn your vehicle around. We're not letting anyone into the medical centre at the moment I'm afraid.'

He hadn't recognised me. It had been at least twenty years.

Before I could explain that Annie was a witness and I'd come to pick her up, he peered at me, frowned, and then his face broke into a beaming smile. 'Frank?'

'Hello, Johnny,' I said, returning his smile.

'How's retirement treating you?' he asked.

'It has its good days,' I replied.

He gave me a meaningful look. 'Someone told me about your wife. I was sorry to hear that she's not well.'

'Thank you.' I gestured to the car park entrance. 'DCI Humphries down there?'

Johnny gave me a forced, sarcastic smile. 'Oh yeah, he's there all right.'

I knew that DCI Dewi Humphries wasn't a popular officer in these parts, and I had very little time for him. In fact, I thought he was an arrogant prick. He'd been a detective sergeant in the North Wales Police when I was still working as a detective inspector. We'd had several run-ins even though I'd been his superior officer. He was just one of those blokes with a huge ego who thought they knew everything and couldn't be told anything. I couldn't stand him, and I knew the feeling was mutual.

'What are you doing here?' Johnny asked.

'I've had a phone call from my friend Annie Taylor,' I explained.

'The judge?'

I nodded. 'Yeah. Apparently, she witnessed the shooting. She's a bit shaken so I'm here to see if she's all right and take her home if she needs me to.'

Johnny thought for a second and then nodded. 'Yeah, no problem, Frank. You might need to let someone from CID know why you're here.'

'Is Kelly Taylor in there?' I asked. I'd encountered DS Kelly Taylor a couple of times in the past six months and, unlike Dewi, I had a lot of time for her. She was a smart, pragmatic copper who was in the job for all the right reasons.

'Yeah,' Johnny replied as he lifted the police tape and gestured for me to drive through.

'Thanks Johnny,' I said as I gave him a friendly wink.

'No problem, Frank. Good to see you looking so well.'

Driving slowly, I saw the blue flashing lights of two patrol cars, an ambulance, and two unmarked CID Astras.

A scene of crime forensics van was parked close to the entrance. Its rear doors were open and several forensic officers in full white nitrile suits, hats, masks and rubber boots were storing evidence inside.

I parked my truck, got out, and scanned the car park looking for Annie.

A white forensic tent had been erected over the body of the GP who had been shot. My mind started to click into detective mode despite my years away from the job. It didn't look like anyone else had been shot, which would suggest that the GP had been deliberately targeted. Why was that?

Then I saw someone waving at me.

It was Annie, and she was sitting on a chair over by where the ambulance was parked. There were two paramedics in high-vis jackets chatting nearby.

'You okay?' I asked as I approached.

Annie nodded as she sipped a mug of tea. 'I've been given the all clear by these lovely paramedics,' she said as she pointed to them.

'What the hell happened?' I asked, lowering my voice to a respectful volume.

Annie shook her head in disbelief. 'I'd just come out of an appointment with Andrew. I was making my way back to my car. He was just over there beside his car on his mobile phone,' she said, pointing over to where the tent was. 'This person seemed to come out of nowhere. They had a gun and they just shot him.'

'That's terrible,' I said with a frown. 'Did you see them?'

'Yes. I saw them from where I was standing. I was about fifteen yards away. But they had a hoodie and mask thing over their face.'

'What type of gun was it?' I asked.

She gave me a knowing look. 'Frank …' she said in a cautionary tone.

'What?' I gave an innocent shrug but I knew exactly what she was thinking. 'I can't help myself. Once a copper, always a copper.'

She sighed. 'Well, if you must know, it was a revolver. Old fashioned.'

I noticed that DS Kelly Taylor was approaching. In her 30s, she was wearing a dark raincoat over her navy suit. Next to her was a male I didn't know. He was about the same age, small framed, dark hair and beard, thick eyebrows and blue eyes.

'How are you feeling now, Annie?' Kelly asked with concern as she arrived.

'A mug of hot sweet tea usually does the trick,' Annie sighed.

Kelly looked at me. 'You two are turning into a bit of a double act.'

I shrugged. 'Annie just rang me to say what had happened.'

Then I gestured over to where Dewi was standing with his hands thrust deep into his pockets, no doubt throwing his weight around and being a generally egotistical tosser. 'Don't worry. I'm just here to make sure that Annie is all right. I'm not going to get in your way on this one.'

Kelly raised an eyebrow. 'Personally, I wouldn't mind if you did, Frank.' She turned to the male next to her. 'I don't think we'd have got to the bottom of Marcus Daniels' death without Frank and Annie getting in the way and taking the time to investigate properly.'

It had been three months since I'd flagged up what appeared to be the suicide of teacher Marcus Daniels as being highly suspicious. Dewi had completely disputed what I'd had to say even though I was vindicated when Marcus' murderer was brought to justice.

I gestured over to Dewi again. 'He's like Teflon, isn't he? I just don't know how he continues to keep his job.'

Kelly gave me a withering smile. 'You know I can't comment on that, Frank.'

I gave her a knowing look. 'Yeah, but I know exactly what you're thinking.'

'This is Detective Constable Ian Ramsey,' Kelly said by way of an introduction. 'He's on secondment from Staffordshire. Literally just arrived.'

Ian blew out his cheeks and shook his head. 'I haven't even been to the station yet. I got the call about the shooting while I was on my way over. Welcome back to North Wales,' he said with dark irony.

'We definitely don't get shootings like this out here very often,' I said.

Kelly then gestured over towards Dewi. 'Oh and Frank, you'll be pleased to hear that the DCI is actually spending some time with the IOPC, so Ian is here to help us out for at least a couple of months.'

The fact that Dewi was finally going to be hauled up in front of the IOPC was music to my ears.

The Independent Office for Police Conduct was the independent complaints watchdog for the English and Welsh Police Force. They investigated the most serious allegations of misconduct by police officers.

'At last,' I said with a dry smile and looked at Ian. 'Hopefully Dolgellau will be down an officer and you'll be here permanently.'

'I wouldn't mind,' he said. 'The weird thing is, I actually grew up around here. And Mum and Dad are here so it's nice being back. I remember my dad talking about you when I was growing up.'

I pulled a face. 'Oh dear.'

'Oh no,' he reassured me, 'it was always good things.'

I looked at him. 'I'm sure I remember you from somewhere, Ian,' I said, trawling my memory.

'Maybe,' he said with a nonchalant shrug. 'We moved away when I was a teenager.'

Kelly looked over at Annie. 'I've taken your preliminary statement. Is there anything else that's occurred to you?'

Annie put the empty mug down on the ground. 'Actually, there is something. The person who shot Andrew.

They were quite small. My initial instinct was that it was a woman.'

Kelly looked shocked. 'A woman?'

'You sound surprised,' I said.

'In my limited experience of shootings, the suspect has always been a man but I'm not ruling anything out,' she admitted.

'At the risk of sounding patronising,' I said, 'the longer you do this job, the more you realise that nothing surprises you.'

'Yeah, that did sound patronising,' Annie teased me, but then her face changed. 'Andrew wasn't married, was he?'

Kelly shook her head. 'No, he wasn't.'

Out of the corner of my eye, I saw a figure approaching.

It was Dewi.

My heart sank as I knew that he'd be unable to be civil or polite.

'Keep calm, Frank,' Annie warned me under her breath.

'Hello Frank,' he said with a forced smile as he puffed out his chest like a moronic pigeon.

'Dewi,' I said through gritted teeth.

He looked at Annie. 'You okay to answer a few more questions?'

Annie nodded.

'You said you saw the suspect driving away?'

'That's right.'

'Did you happen to see if they took the firearm back to the car with them?'

'No, sorry. I was crouched on the ground at that point.'

'It was a revolver though,' I stated.

Kelly seemed surprised. 'Definitely a revolver?' she asked to confirm.

Annie nodded. 'I've seen my fair share of firearms over the years. It was definitely a revolver. Longish barrel. Say seven or eight inches.'

'Maybe a service revolver,' I suggested, thinking out loud. As a police officer, many of the guns I'd encountered had originated from the 1950s and 1960s when soldiers, especially officers, made a habit of keeping their Webley service handguns.

'Those days are long gone, Frank,' Dewi said with a derisive snort as he looked back at Annie. 'And this person took Andrew's wallet and his briefcase?'

'Yes.'

'Sounds like a robbery gone wrong,' he said.

'Robbery?' I scoffed. 'This isn't South London. It was a deliberate attack, not a random robbery.'

Dewi gave me a withering look. 'The world has changed quite a lot since you were an officer, Frank. But thanks for your thoughts, however out of date they are.'

I ignored him for a few seconds.

'I hear you're off across the border for a bit, Dewi?' I said with a smirk. I just couldn't help myself.

He visibly bristled, shoved his hands into his pockets and grumbled, 'Right, I'm going to see what the SOCOs have found.'

I glanced over to Annie. 'Ready to go?'

She stood up slowly and nodded. 'Yes. I've had quite enough trauma for one day.'

Chapter 4

I pulled up outside Annie's detached house and stopped the truck. Understandably, she'd been very quiet on the journey back. *Rocky Mountain High* by *John Denver* was playing very softly on the car stereo. We sat for over a minute just listening to the music. The soft, haunting voice, the lilting guitar, the sad lyrics. Then I turned to look at her but she was still lost deep in thought.

'Are you going to be okay?' I asked with genuine concern. Seeing someone being shot and killed was incredibly traumatic for anyone. And Annie seemed to have genuinely liked Andrew Burrows.

She nodded. 'I think so.' Then she met my eyes. 'I just don't understand why anyone would want to do that to Andrew.' She was clearly upset.

'Did you know him well?' I asked.

'Not really, but he'd been my GP for the past couple of years and he was lovely. Kind and gentle. And I know he'd done some really good work in the local community. It just doesn't make any sense.'

'No, it doesn't,' I agreed.

She then gave me a knowing look. 'I filmed the person who shot him as they drove away,' she said, getting her phone out of her pocket.

I held her gaze for a moment. 'Did you tell the police that?'

She pulled a face to signify that she hadn't.

'Why not?' I asked, more out of curiosity than judgement.

'After the fiasco with my sister, and then what happened with Marcus Daniels, my trust in Dolgellau CID to do a thorough job is very questionable.'

I knew what she meant. The police investigation into her sister Meg's murder six months ago had been so shambolic that the IOPC was looking again at an investigation into three historic murders in the late 90s in North Wales. A man named Keith Tatchell had been convicted of the murders at the time, despite protesting his innocence. Three months ago, it had been revealed that the murders had actually been carried out by Annie's husband, Stephen. I knew that Dewi and the senior investigating officer, DCI Ian Goddard, had cut corners and possibly fabricated evidence to secure the conviction of Tatchell. How Dewi hadn't been suspended for this, I had no idea. I was just glad that he was now going to have to account for all his decision-making and actions to the IOPC.

'Yes, I completely agree,' I said. 'Trusting them to do anything properly is a mistake. But keeping key evidence from them might be seen as obstruction or even perverting the course of justice.'

Annie gave me a funny look. 'That doesn't sound like you, Frank. You're normally happy to bend the law to breaking point.'

It was a fair point. I just didn't want her to get into trouble.

'Anyway, they didn't ask. How can it be obstruction?'

I gave an ironic laugh. 'They didn't ask you if you just happened to film the suspect driving away from the crime scene? That is sloppy of them.'

Annie smirked. She knew I was being ironic. 'Anyway, I'm not sure why we're debating all this,' she sighed as she started to tap on her phone. Then she showed me the video clip. 'Here we go.'

The shaky video showed a silver VW Golf driving past at speed. However, it was impossible to see much more than that.

'Can you slow it down?' I asked.

'I think so.' Annie took out her glasses, popped them on, and then peered at her phone. 'Isn't there a slow motion thingy button?'

I sighed. 'Mmm, I think you're asking the wrong person. I was under the impression that my phone's primary purpose was to make phone calls.'

She cast a scornful look in my direction. 'Really? You complete luddite.'

'Charming,' I joked.

'Here we go.' She replayed the footage of the silver Golf driving past.

Then she paused it.

I peered at it again. 'Shame we can't see inside the car or who's driving it.'

She nodded in agreement. 'At least we can see the reg.'

The car's licence plate was clearly visible – *GH11 BNB.*

'I'll see if Ethan can help us out with that. Maybe we can track down the registered owner.'

'Useful to have a grandson with tech skills,' I said.

Annie got out of the truck and then sighed. 'Ten weeks ago, he didn't even know I was his grandmother.'

'How's all that going?' I asked.

She shrugged and then smiled. 'It's going very well actually. All three of us are closer than ever now that there are no more secrets.'

'Good for you,' I said with genuine joy. I could see how much it meant to Annie and I was pleased for her. 'If you need to chat later, ring me. Any time.'

She gave me a smile. 'I know I've said it before, but you're one of the good ones, Frank Marshal.'

I shrugged. I wasn't comfortable getting any sort of compliment. 'I don't know about that.'

Then she looked directly at me. 'You think you can help me find out who did this to Andrew?'

I nodded. 'Of course.'

'I'll see you tomorrow, Frank.'

I watched her walk up to her front door with the slightest of limps. As she put the key in the door she turned to me and rolled her eyes. 'Not very dignified, walking with a limp, is it?'

'I don't know,' I said with a grin. 'I think it suits you.'

She gave me a two-fingered salute and laughed. 'I'll let you know what Ethan comes up with.'

Then she went inside.

For a moment, I thought about what Annie had told me about Meredith. In 1967, Annie had become pregnant after a drunken one-night stand. She was seventeen. Her daughter, Meredith, had been given up for adoption. In 2007, Meredith had contacted Annie. She was a single mum with a 16-year-old son, Ethan. After a few tense meetings, Annie and Meredith agreed that they wanted to be in each other's lives. However, Annie hadn't told a soul about who Meredith or Ethan were until very recently.

I started the truck's engine.

Take Me Home, Country Roads by *John Denver* was now playing on the stereo.

As I pulled away, I turned up the volume and started to hum, deep in thought. 'West Virginia, mountain mama …'

Chapter 5

I placed a tray with a mug of tea and a plate of biscuits down beside Rachel. 'Here you go.'

'Oh, you are a dear,' she said, her eyes smiling up at me.

'I am a dear, you're right,' I replied, and smiled back.

It was a little exchange, a funny little saying, that went back many years when we brought stuff to each other. It felt reassuring to hear her say it.

Biting into the chocolate hobnob, Rachel frowned. 'Ooh, these are nice, Frank. What are they?'

'Dark chocolate hobnobs,' I said. 'They're your favourite.'

'Are they?' she asked, looking confused.

I sat down in the armchair that was next to hers, took my whiskey and rolled the ice cube around it. I loved the sound it made as it whizzed around the cut glass tumbler. I took a sip and savoured the earthy, spicy flavour.

'What are we watching?' I asked as a I gestured to the television.

'*Vera*,' Rachel replied. It was one of her favourite TV

programmes. However, I had sadly noticed that she was finding it increasingly difficult to follow the clues and twists and turns of the plot.

'How's Caitlin?' she asked.

It had only been three months since my daughter's partner, TJ, a feckless minor drug dealer, had turned up here brandishing a knife in the middle of the night. He'd banged loudly on the front door of the annexe of our farmhouse, demanding to see my grandson, Sam. My daughter, Caitlin, had left TJ and their home in North London only a few days earlier after he'd hit her. It was my assumption that it wasn't the first time he'd been physically abusive towards her by any stretch of the imagination. Brandishing my shotgun, I'd eventually managed to overpower him, get the knife from him, and waited for the police to arrive.

Caitlin and Sam now lived over in the annexe to the farmhouse and had started to build new lives for themselves. We'd found Sam a local school and he was thriving.

'She's fine,' I said. 'She and Sam are both fine.'

I could tell from Rachel's pensive expression that she couldn't remember who Sam was, even though he'd been sitting with her about two hours ago.

'Sam's our grandson,' I said gently. 'Remember?'

'Of course I remember,' she scoffed.

I knew that she didn't.

Chapter 6

I'd picked Annie up at 9am. Our plan was to go and talk to Sally Partridge, an old acquaintance of hers. She was a part-time receptionist at the medical centre, and we wanted to see what she could tell us about Andrew Burrows. We were still convinced that his shooting wasn't a robbery gone wrong, and that the motive was more personal. Annie had rung the centre and discovered that Sally wasn't working today so we were going to see her at her home.

However, I wanted to check something else out before we made our way there. For the past few weeks, Caitlin's scumbag of an ex-partner TJ had vanished from the area. Three months ago, I'd placed a GPS tracking device on his car so that I could keep an eye on his movements. He had made it known that he had no intention of returning to London without my grandson, Sam. And I had no intention of letting him anywhere near either of them.

Annie and I had discovered that he was selling firearms, using the local woods as a test shooting range. Having handed this information to DS Kelly Thomas, the last I'd heard was that TJ was under the surveillance of the National Crime Agency. But when the GPS tracker stopped working, I was forced to go over to his house to see what had happened and possibly replace it, hoping that he hadn't discovered it and removed it himself. That's when I'd realised that he had moved out of the property and disappeared. And now I had no way of tracking his movements. I prayed that he'd got bored of living out in the middle of Snowdonia/Eryri and had returned to London. But I needed to know for certain.

Pulling up outside *Rose Cottage*, I saw to my relief that the scruffy drive was still empty. The shutters at all the windows were still closed just as they had been the last time I visited.

'Looks pretty deserted to me,' Annie said as she opened the passenger door.

'Fingers crossed,' I said as I jumped out of my truck. 'You can stay here if you want.'

Annie frowned. 'I'm not a bloody geriatric, Frank. I've got a sore knee,' she growled.

I held up my hands in mock defence. 'Okay. Sorry. You did have a bit of a day of it yesterday.'

'I'm fine,' she snapped. 'Stop fussing.'

We walked across the narrow, leaf-strewn road to the isolated cottage.

'Anyone tell you that you're getting cranky in your old age?' I joked.

'I'm ignoring you,' she said with a smile.

I went to a ground floor window, cupped my hands, and peered through a small crack in the blind.

The shadowy kitchen was empty – not even a kettle or toaster on the counter.

Annie wandered across to the other side of the cottage.

'This would make a lovely home for someone if it was spruced up a bit.'

I nodded in agreement, but I was distracted by my concern that I didn't know where TJ *was*. It made me feel uneasy.

'Frank,' Annie said in a concerned tone.

I looked over and saw that she was now standing on the driveway.

'What is it?' I asked as I marched over to see what she'd found.

She gestured to something lying on the edge of the grass and the drive.

It was the GPS tracking device. And it had been smashed into pieces.

I sighed in frustration. 'Looks like he did find it.'

Chapter 7

Twenty minutes later, Annie and I walked up the neat pathway through Sally Partridge's front garden to her small bungalow. Over to our right, there were compact and curvy Veronica bushes, and a huge oak tree with thick, gnarled branches. There was an old brick archway about halfway along, and the sandy-coloured bricks were worn and pitted so that they no longer had edges or corners.

Arriving at the porch, I saw that the tiles, painted wooden balustrade, and front door itself were immaculately clean.

Annie knocked on the door, took a step back and winced. I pretended not to notice as she would only grumble that I was 'fussing' again.

A few seconds later, the front door opened and a sharp-featured woman in her early 40s, glasses, dark kaftan, peered out at us.

'Annie?' she said.

'Hi Sally,' Annie said apologetically. 'I'm so sorry to disturb you but I wondered if you had five minutes?'

'Erm, yes. Of course.' Sally looked confused but ushered us in anyway.

'This is my friend, Frank,' Annie explained.

Sally gave Annie a compassionate look. 'How are you doing? Someone told me you saw what happened to Andrew yesterday and that it happened right in front of you.'

'Yes, I'm afraid so. It was incredibly shocking.'

'Do you want to come in?' Sally asked, gesturing behind her.

'Thank you,' I said with a kind smile. 'We won't take more than a few minutes.'

'Come on through,' she said.

The living room was neat and fastidiously tidy. I immediately spotted there were no signs of children in the hallway or anywhere else. If I was to guess, Sally lived on her own in the bungalow.

Annie and I sat down on the large coffee-coloured sofa while Sally lowered herself into a large armchair with a floral pattern. If I hadn't seen that Sally was in her 40s, I might have guessed that the bungalow was occupied by someone a lot older. It smelled of lavender and furniture polish.

'And how are *you* doing?' Annie asked Sally.

She shook her head and sighed, deep in thought. 'It's such a shock. It doesn't feel real. I don't understand why someone would do that just to get a wallet and Andrew's briefcase. This sort of thing just doesn't happen around here.'

Annie leaned forward. 'That's why we wanted to talk to you actually.'

Sally gave an audible tut to herself. 'I'm so sorry. Where are my manners? Would you like a coffee or tea?'

'We're fine, but thank you,' I said.

'I'm just walking around in a bit of a daze today,' Sally admitted as she blinked her eyes.

'Of course,' Annie said. 'You see, Frank here is a retired detective ...'

'I thought I recognised you from somewhere,' Sally said with a nod. 'You used to drink and play darts with my Uncle Derek years ago.'

'That's right. I was sorry to hear that he's no longer with us.' What I didn't like to say is that Derek Partridge drank ten pints and smoked forty fags every day for as long as I knew him. The fact that he reached sixty-one years old was a bloody miracle.

'Thank you,' Sally said.

'The thing is,' Annie continued, 'we're not convinced that Andrew's death was a robbery.'

Sally narrowed her eyes. 'I don't understand. That's what the police said had happened.'

I rubbed my beard for a second. 'I worked as a police officer for thirty years, and Annie was a judge for the same period. We've never encountered an armed robbery in North Wales where one person has been attacked. Andrew Burrows wasn't a particularly wealthy man. Why shoot him dead in a car park just to take his wallet? It doesn't make any sense.'

Sally paused for a second as she processed what I'd said. 'When you put it like that, it does sound very strange. It's not like we're living in some ghetto in America is it? But I'd heard a rumour that it was some drug addict who needed money for drugs.'

Annie moved a strand of hair from her face. 'Sally, I saw the person who killed Andrew. I watched as they came over and shot him at close range to make sure he was dead, and I have no doubts that he was targeted and that it was personal.'

Sally looked upset and a little lost by all that we'd told her. 'Oh my goodness, I didn't know that.'

'We were wondering if Andrew had had any arguments or disputes with patients or the family of a patient in recent weeks or months?'

She shook her head immediately. 'No. Nothing like that.' But even as she said it, her face changed as if she'd thought of something.

'Whatever it is, Sally,' Annie said, spotting this, 'it might really help us.'

'I don't really want to say but ...' Sally said, struggling.

'Please,' I encouraged her. 'Whatever you tell us, we won't reveal where the information came from.'

She took a breath and nodded as if to signal that she had decided to tell us. 'We had a poor little boy, Joseph Reeves. He was only eight years old when he first came to see us.'

'And Andrew was his doctor?' I asked to clarify.

'Yes, that's right. His mother, Sian, said that she thought he'd twisted his knee playing football. Andrew examined him and there were no other symptoms so he just strapped it up. But the pain in his leg got worse. Andrew saw him again and thought that he'd torn the ligaments. Eventually, Joseph was sent for an MRI scan on his leg, along with other tests, and he was diagnosed with leukaemia.'

'Oh God,' Annie said under her breath.

'Joseph was incredibly brave but he eventually died three months ago in a local hospice,' Sally explained.

'Did the family blame Andrew for this?' I asked, joining up the dots.

'Yes. Well, Joseph's father, Tom Reeves did. In fact, he came to the medical centre to confront Andrew about two months ago. It all kicked off in the car park.'

'Do you mean that Tom Reeves attacked Andrew?' Annie asked.

Sally shook her head. 'No, nothing like that. Tom was with his brother and sister, and Judy went out to calm it all down.'

I scratched at my beard. 'Judy?' I asked.

'Judy Thompson. She's one of the partner GPs at the practice. She threatened to call the police if they didn't leave. There's been nothing like that since.'

'Thank you. That's very useful,' I said.

I glanced at Annie. We needed to consider Tom Reeves as a viable suspect.

Chapter 8

Annie and I had pulled up in the Marian Cefn Car Park which overlooked Dolgellau Rugby Club. For a moment I remembered bringing my son James down here when he was about ten or eleven to play mini rugby. It didn't last more than a few weeks. James didn't enjoy it but I didn't blame him. I'd always preferred football myself. James just wasn't aggressive or determined enough to ever play competitive sport, but that was fine with me. I just wanted him to enjoy what he was doing, which wasn't the attitude of some of the other parents who would berate their sons from the touchline.

Annie was peering at her phone screen. 'Okay, I think I've got something,' she said, breaking my train of thought. 'Tom Reeves is part owner of a garage on the road out towards Bontnewydd.'

Bontnewydd was a tiny village about ten minutes' drive away. 'Yeah, I think I know where that is. Just before you get to Dolgamedd Holiday Park.'

I turned on the engine and clicked the stereo. *Do It Again* by *Steely Dan* started to play.

Annie gave me a quizzical look. '*Steely Dan?*'

'What?' I said defensively as I pulled out of the car park and started to head towards the A494.

She chuckled. 'I didn't know you liked *Steely Dan.*'

'Why is that so funny?' I asked.

'I don't know. I just had you down as a country man through and through.'

'I have a very eclectic taste in music, I'll have you know,' I announced.

'Yes, okay,' she said dubiously.

The sky above us was bright blue and dotted with huge white clouds. A plane had left a sharp, white vapor trail across the sky as it headed west. I wondered where it was going.

Annie followed my gaze up into the sky. 'Ireland or America?'

'Got to be America.'

'You ever been?' she asked.

I shook my head. 'Sadly, no. Rachel and I always promised each other we'd go. A little tour. Start in Nashville and the Grand Ole Opry. Down to Memphis and Graceland. Then onto New Orleans.' As I said this, I could feel the sense of loss and regret that suddenly came over me.

'Maybe one day,' Annie said. 'You're still young.'

I looked over at her. 'But not with Rachel.'

'No,' she said gently. 'How's she doing, if that's not a silly question?'

I pulled out onto the other side of the road and overtook an idling caravan.

'It's not a silly question,' I reassured her. 'It just feels as if she's being slowly chipped away, week by week. Because I'm with her every day, I don't always notice it. But then I remember that something she could do, or say, or remember last month has now changed or gone.'

Annie reached across and lightly touched my forearm. 'That's so hard. For the both of you,' she said empathetically.

'Having Caitlin and Sam next door has been a godsend for both of us,' I admitted.

We drove for a minute or two in a thoughtful silence before I saw the garage looming on the right-hand side of the road up ahead of us.

'Here we go,' I said, gesturing as I turned into the small customers' car park of the ramshackle garage.

A large rusty sign that had seen better days said *MOT, SERVICE, REPAIRS*.

There were two inspection pits that had cars up on the hydraulic jacks.

We got out and made our way over to a small building that had a sign above the door – *CUSTOMERS*.

The small office, reception and waiting room was dark and smelled of cigarette smoke and coffee. There were a couple of red plastic chairs and an old coffee machine to our right, and a few dog-eared car magazines were scattered on a low table.

A woman in her 50s – ruddy complexion, bleach blonde hair and thick make-up – looked up at us from behind a desk.

'Yes, dear. How can I help?' she asked in a friendly voice as Annie took a step forward.

'Is Tom about?' she asked.

The woman frowned. 'He's not in, love. Can I help?'

'My son brought my car in yesterday and Tom did a basic service on it,' Annie explained, lying through her teeth. I admired her ability to sound so convincing in situations like these. 'I think he forgot to put the locking nut back in the glove box. I just wanted to check if it was here by any chance or if he'd seen it.'

The woman narrowed her eyes. 'Sorry. Are you sure Tom did the service on your car? It's just that he wasn't in yesterday.'

Annie gave me a surreptitious look.

'Oh. I'm sure it was yesterday, but if he wasn't in maybe I've got it wrong,' she said with an embarrassed laugh. 'So, Tom's not going to be in today?'

'No.'

'Oh. Is he all right?' Annie said, sounding concerned.

'Just a personal matter. Friend of yours, is he?'

'Sort of,' Annie replied.

The woman pulled over a large book and turned the pages back. 'If you give me the registration number, I can have a look and see when we serviced the car.'

Annie gave me a quizzical look. 'I've just got it and I know this sounds stupid but I can't for the life of me remember the registration.'

I shook my head. 'Neither can I.'

The woman laughed. 'You'd be surprised the number of people who come in here and don't know their registration. Look, Tom should be back in tomorrow.' Then she gestured outside. 'Or you could ask one of the lads if they've seen it.'

'Thank you. I'll pop back tomorrow,' Annie said with a friendly smile as we turned and went outside.

We headed back towards the car.

'Okay, so he wasn't in work yesterday or today,' I said, thinking out loud. Then I had a thought. I fished my leather wallet out of my coat pocket. 'Actually, just wait there for a second.'

'Why? Where are you going?'

'Trust me,' I said as I turned and headed over to where

the mechanics were working on a car that was jacked up about head height.

'Yes, you've said that before,' Annie joked.

As I reached the inspection pit, a man in his 20s with coal black hair looked over at me. 'Can I help?'

I held up my wallet. 'Yeah. Tom Reeves left his wallet in the pub last night. I popped in to give it back to him but he's not here.'

'You were in the Ship?' the man asked.

'That's right,' I said. 'Don't suppose you've got an address so I can drop it back to him?'

'Yeah, no problem. I'll just go and scribble it down for you, pal.'

'Thanks.'

I turned to look at Annie who gave me an amused look and shook her head.

Chapter 9

Ten minutes later, Annie and I pulled up outside a small terraced house in a narrow street in the middle of Dolgellau. The house was constructed from grey dolerite and slate, in a style that was unique to the town.

'What's our story now?' Annie asked as she unfastened her seatbelt.

'Collecting for *Help The Aged*?' I joked.

'Very funny,' she sighed.

As I got out, I noticed that the house to the right of the address we'd been given for Tom Reeves was for sale.

I looked at Annie and gave her an impish smile. 'It's okay, I've got this,' I reassured her as we walked up the pavement to the front door and rang the doorbell.

A few seconds later, a woman in her 30s with bright ginger curly hair and freckles opened the door and peered out at us. She had a friendly face and intelligent green eyes.

'Hello?' she said.

'Oh hi,' I said in a jovial voice. 'I'm Frank and this is my wife, Annie.' Then I gestured to the house next door. 'We've just put in an offer on this house so I thought we'd introduce ourselves as it looks like we're going to be neighbours.'

'Oh right. I'm Carol,' she said, reaching out and shaking our hands. 'Come in.'

'Oh, we don't want to interrupt you if you're in the middle of doing stuff,' Annie said.

'No, no. It's fine,' she replied in a soft voice. 'Come on in.'

We went inside to a tiny hallway and then Carol guided us into a small living room.

On the mantelpiece there was a series of photos of a young boy who I assumed was her son, Joseph, who had died recently. It was heartbreaking to see his little face smiling in those photos and I couldn't help but think of Sam. I couldn't bear it if anything ever happened to him.

'That's Joseph,' Carol said as she spotted me looking. 'We lost him just over three months ago to leukaemia.'

'Oh no. I'm so sorry to hear that,' I said gently. There was now part of me that felt incredibly guilty about going in there on a false pretence.

'That's terrible,' Annie said in a virtual whisper.

There was a poignant silence.

Glancing at a family photo, I saw Carol and Joseph with a large, bearded man who I assumed was Tom.

'That must be so difficult for you and your husband,' I said with a nod towards the photo.

'It's been incredibly difficult for us,' Carol answered, her voice full of emotion.

'I think I recognise your husband from somewhere,' I said of the photo.

'Tom?'

'Yes.'

'He's a mechanic at Jacksons garage. Maybe you've seen him there?'

'Yes. I've used Jacksons before so that must be it.'

'It would have been nice to meet him,' Annie said, 'but I guess he's at work today.'

Carol shook her head with a sad expression. 'Actually, he's at another funeral. We're in a charity support group for families who have children with cancer. We lost poor Eve last week who lived just up the road here. She was only fifteen. Tom's at the wake in The Old Ship. I couldn't bring myself to go after everything we'd gone through with Joseph.'

'Sorry to hear that,' Annie said as she got up and winced at the pain in her knee. 'We'll meet him next time.'

'And I'm sorry we've intruded at such a difficult time,' I added. There was nothing about Carol's manner that was at all suspicious, but then again, she didn't know that we were looking into Andrew Burrow's murder.

'Not at all.' she said as she saw us to the front door. 'Well, it was very nice to meet you. I hope your offer's successful.'

'Yes, me too,' I said as we went out of the front door and headed for the car.

Chapter 10

Annie and I now sat in the truck in the car park of The Royal Ship pub in Dolgellau. It was a two-minute drive from where we'd parked outside Carol Reeves' house.

'That felt very awkward, didn't it?' I admitted, as we hadn't really spoken on the brief journey.

'Yes. I felt we were intruding on her grief,' Annie agreed, 'and seeing her son on those photos really brought it home.'

I turned to look at Annie. 'You saw the person who shot Andrew Burrows yesterday, and you said that you thought it might have been a woman. What did you think?'

She shook her head. 'I'm not sure. My instinct is that she's too tall to be the person I saw. That's what made it feel uncomfortable being in her house, talking about her son, knowing that we were there on a false pretext.'

'And unless Tom Reeves turns out to be shorter and smaller than her,' I said, 'then we're back to square one.'

'Maybe it's one of their relatives?' she suggested.

'Maybe.'

Then something occurred to me which Annie and I hadn't discussed.

'I've just thought of something,' I said.

Annie raised an eyebrow quizzically. 'Would you like to share it?'

'The person who shot Andrew took the time not only to take his wallet, but also his briefcase,' I said, thinking aloud.

'Yes,' Annie said as she processed this.

'My assumption was that they took the wallet to make it look like a robbery.'

'That was my assumption too,' Annie agreed and then frowned. 'But why go to the trouble of taking his briefcase too?'

'This is a stretch, but was there something in that briefcase that the suspect wanted? Maybe I'm clutching at straws?'

'No, I think it's a good point.'

My concentration was broken as a few mourners, who were dressed in black, left the pub. None of them bore any resemblance to Tom Reeves though.

'Thing is,' I said, 'there's no way of us finding out what was in that briefcase.'

I looked up and saw several more mourners coming out of the pub.

One of them was a huge, bearded man who had to be about 6'4".

It was Tom Reeves.

'I think that's him, isn't it?' I asked with a nod in his direction.

Annie nodded. 'Yes, and there's no way he was the person I saw shoot Andrew yesterday.'

Chapter 11

'Here you go,' Annie said as she placed a mug of tea in front of me.

We'd been sitting at her kitchen table for about an hour trawling through Andrew Burrows' social media and anything else we could find on the internet that might be relevant.

'Thanks,' I said as I studied Andrew's Facebook profile. 'The only thing I can see is that he was a very popular, sociable, and sporty man who had a loving family. But then again, people don't really advertise their darkest secrets on social media, do they?'

'No,' Annie agreed as she sat down. 'They don't.'

'Any danger of a biscuit?' I asked with a cheeky grin.

She shook her head. 'There's not a biscuit in the house anymore. I'm trying to stop eating sugar and trans fats. Ironically it was Andrew who did a blood test and told me that I was pre-diabetic and to cut down on stuff like biscuits.'

I sighed. 'You ever get the feeling that medical progress

is stopping anyone having any pleasure in life? A biscuit is a bloody biscuit, isn't it?'

Annie shrugged. 'Apparently not.' Before we could continue, her phone rang. 'It's Ethan,' she said, pointing to the caller ID on the screen. We were still waiting to see if he could find anything out about the VW Golf that Annie had seen the killer driving away in.

'Hi Ethan,' she said as she put her phone onto speaker. 'I'm putting you on speaker. Frank's with me.'

'Hey Frank,' Ethan said cheerfully.

'Hi Ethan.'

'I've done some digging on the registration, Gran,' Ethan said in an amused tone.

Annie huffed loudly. 'I wish you wouldn't call me that,' she groaned. 'I don't mind Nain?'

'How about 'Granny'?' he suggested.

I snorted into my tea. Although Annie had never struck me as vain, I think she drew the line at being called 'Gran' or 'Granny'.

'Ethan!' she said abruptly.

'Sorry. Anyway, turns out that the plate on that car is false. According to the DVLA database, that registration just doesn't exist and never has done.'

'Bugger,' I said under my breath in frustration.

'Sorry not to have better news on that one,' he continued, 'but I did run a check. If we assume that the year of the plate is correct, then there are only seven silver VW Golfs registered in a 50-mile radius of Dolgellau. Bit of a longshot, I know. Do you want me to email over the list of owners?'

'Please,' Annie said.

'I'm going to run that video you took through some software to see if we can get a clearer image of the driver,' he added. 'Of course, they were probably still wearing a mask at the time.'

'Probably, but that would be great,' I said. 'Anything that might narrow it down.'

'Okay. I'm on it. I'll let you know how I get on.'

'I'll come and see you soon,' Annie said as she ended the call and looked at me. 'He's a little bugger.'

I smiled and nodded, but something had popped up on my screen that caught my attention.

Welsh-based doctor claims that statins are being over-prescribed and are unnecessary for millions of patients looking to lower their cholesterol.

'What is it?' Annie asked, noticing my change of expression.

I pointed to the screen. 'Article about Andrew Burrows in *The Sunday Times* from January of this year.'

'About what?'

I skim-read the article for a few seconds. 'According to this, Andrew had spent five years researching the prescribing of statins in the UK. His conclusion was that doctors were over-prescribing them and that the vast majority of patients with high cholesterol could, and should, change their diet and use exercise to control it instead. He had an article about his findings published in two medical journals last year.'

'Okay,' Annie said with a furrowed brow, 'but I'm not sure I follow you.'

'Last year, a major pharmaceutical company tried to take legal action against him for being a statin-denier and for disseminating dangerous misinformation about the use of statins that they claimed was incredibly dangerous for public health,' I said as I continued to read from the article. 'A major UK newspaper published an article disparaging Andrew's research and calling him 'a dangerous quack'. Andrew countered with a defamation claim against the newspaper that is still tied up in court.'

'You think someone shot him because of his research?' Annie asked, not convinced.

'I've no idea, but if we're going on the hypothesis that he was targeted, we're still searching for a clear motive.'

'But we haven't ruled out someone from Joseph Reeves' family yet, have we? It could have been Carol Reeves,' Annie pointed out.

'No, I get that,' I agreed, 'but I go on the principle of exploring every possible line of enquiry until we can close it down.'

'Sounds sensible. And you're the expert in detection.'

'Can I have that in writing?' I asked, teasing her.

She laughed. 'No.'

'Anyway, listen to this. Statins are one of the most lucrative drugs in the history of medicine. It's a trillion-dollar industry,' I said as I ran my finger over the article. 'There are eight million people taking statins in the UK. It's worth £500 million a year.'

'And if someone can prove that the drug is being over-prescribed and unnecessary in many cases, that's a big motive to want that person to be silenced,' Annie said.

I shrugged. 'I don't know. But I think it has to be worth looking at.'

'We should go tomorrow and talk to one of the other GPs at the medical centre and see what they can tell us,' Annie suggested.

I nodded in agreement, but before I could say anything else, my phone rang.

It was Caitlin.

'Hi,' I said, as I answered. 'Everything okay at home?' Part of me still worried that TJ was going to turn up at the farmhouse at some point. But Caitlin had a shotgun and

Jack to scare most people off and I was only a ten-minute drive away.

'It's Mum,' Caitlin said, sounding a little frantic.

'What's wrong?' I asked anxiously.

'She's sitting in my car and she's refusing to get out.'

'Okay. I'll be there in fifteen minutes,' I said as I ended the call and then looked over at Annie. 'I've got to go.'

Chapter 12

Jumping out of my truck, I jogged up the track to where Caitlin's car was parked. She and Sam were standing outside the car. I could see that Rachel was sitting in the passenger seat.

'What's going on?' I asked quietly as I approached.

'Mum says that she wants to go to the house in Llanbedrog,' Caitlin explained. 'I've told her that you guys sold it about ten years ago but she won't listen to me.'

Rachel and I had inherited a tiny cottage from her parents that we then used for a while as a holiday home.

'Okay, let me talk to her,' I said, trying to reassure her. I could see that Caitlin was getting upset.

Sam looked up at me. 'Is Nain going to be all right?'

I nodded and patted his shoulder. 'Yes, mate. She's going to be fine. She's just a bit confused, that's all. Nothing to worry about.' Then I looked at Caitlin. 'You guys go inside or you're going to get cold.'

Caitlin gestured to the car. 'I offered Mum a blanket but she didn't want one. She must be shivering in there.'

I crouched down and looked at Rachel through the open passenger window.

'Hi love,' I said in a gentle voice. 'Everything okay?'

'Not really,' she snapped angrily. 'I've asked Caitlin to take me to the house at Llanbedrog but she won't. I don't know what the matter is with her. She loves it there.'

I took a moment to compose myself. 'We sold that house a few years ago. Do you remember?' I said softly.

'Don't be ridiculous, Frank,' Rachel said, pulling a face. 'Come on. If we go now, we can get there before it gets dark. And where on earth is James? He should be back by now.'

I looked at Rachel's slightly manic expression, searching for the woman that I'd married. This was by far the worst episode of dementia that I'd witnessed since she'd been diagnosed with Lewy Bodies. She'd had the odd hallucination at night, along with remembering phone calls or snippets of information that just hadn't happened, but her dementia seemed to have ramped up a notch. My heart sank as I looked at her bewildered face. She just didn't know that our beautiful son had taken his own life just over ten years ago. And she couldn't remember that we'd sold her parents' cottage just after that. What made this worse was the knowledge that her behaviour and memory was only going to decline in the coming months and years.

I took a long, deep breath as a wave of emotion came over me. 'James isn't here.'

'Where is he?' she asked, shaking her head. 'I thought he was coming with us. And where has Caitlin gone?'

'I tell you what,' I said very quietly and calmly. 'I've still got to pack my stuff up.'

Rachel looked genuinely puzzled. 'I thought you did that this morning, Frank,' she said with a big sigh.

DEADLY CARE

'No. I had to go out, remember?' I said, trying to play along. There was no point in contradicting her with what she was saying. In her mind, it was true. Reality and logic didn't come into it.

'Okay. Well, I'll stay here then,' she said, folding her arms and sounding a little like a grumpy child.

'Are you sure? Because it's getting pretty chilly out here. I've got an idea. Let's go inside and I'll make us a nice cup of tea. And I've got some biscuits. Dark chocolate hobnobs.'

'Oh yes, I like those,' she said, but she still looked a little suspicious at what I was saying.

'You come and have a cup of tea and a biscuit and keep warm. I'll pack up my stuff and then we'll drive over to Llanbedrog,' I said slowly. 'How does that sound?'

'Yes. I think that sounds like a good plan, Frank.' With that, she opened the door with such a sudden movement so that I had to move out of the way to avoid being hit.

'Come on then, love,' I said reassuringly. I put my hand on her shoulder and guided her from Caitlin's car back towards our farmhouse.

Out of the corner of my eye, I saw Caitlin standing in the doorway.

I gave her a weary, slightly sad, thumbs up. 'She's going to be fine,' I said.

Chapter 13

'Mrs Taylor?' said a voice at the Dolgellau Medical Centre.

Annie had used her charm to get us an emergency appointment with Dr Judy Thompson, the senior partner.

Judy was in her 30s, with brunette hair that fell onto her shoulders, an intelligent face, and a no-nonsense manner.

'Hello Annie,' she said before giving me a slightly suspicious look.

'This is my friend Frank,' Annie explained. 'Is it okay if he comes in with me for a bit of moral support?'

'Of course.' Judy led us down the small corridor and into her consulting room. 'Please, take a seat.' She sat down at her desk and turned her swivel chair to face Annie, while I perched on the spare chair near the door. 'You were here the day before yesterday and you saw Andrew, is that right?'

'Yes. Actually, I saw him being ... attacked outside.'

'Oh gosh. That's terrible,' Judy said with a well-rehearsed empathetic expression. 'It must have been such a shock. Is that why you're here this morning? It can take a while to get over seeing a traumatic event like that, so I can prescribe a sedative to help you sleep and something for anxiety if you need it?'

Annie took her time before replying. 'I'm going to come clean. Frank and I are actually here because we don't think that Andrew's death was a robbery gone wrong.'

Judy looked at both of us with a wary puzzlement. 'I'm not sure that I understand.'

'I used to work as a detective,' I told her, hoping that she wasn't going to get angry at our deception and throw us out immediately. 'In thirty years of being on the job, I've never known anyone to be shot three times at close range for their wallet and briefcase. It just doesn't happen in North Wales.'

She thought about what I'd said for a moment and then sighed. For a few seconds, I was concerned that she was going to tell us to get out.

Then she said, 'It's something that's been troubling me too. The police said it might have been drug addicts, but it just didn't add up when I thought about it.'

Annie leaned back in her chair. 'I agree. The person who shot Andrew was very calm and focussed. And once he was on the ground they shot him twice more to make sure he was dead. It was personal. Andrew was targeted.'

'Do the police know this is what you saw?' Judy asked, her eyebrows raised in question.

'Yes, and that's what makes this so frustrating.'

'I understand your concern, but why do you want to speak to me this morning? I didn't see anything.'

'We're aware that Andrew had been doing a lot of research into the use of statins,' I explained. 'Or rather the over-prescription of statins.'

Judy pulled a face. 'Oh that. Yes, to say that he had

ruffled a few feathers would be an understatement. That's why he got a job down here two years ago.'

Annie sat forward. 'I don't understand.'

'Andrew is ... or was ... a very well-respected cardiologist. But when he wrote his paper exposing what he perceived to be the overuse of statins, he made a lot of enemies.'

'With the pharmaceutical companies?' I asked.

'Yes, but also with many top doctors who didn't agree with what he was saying. He was blacklisted from working in a lot of hospitals.'

'What did you think?' Annie asked.

'I thought what Andrew was saying was very valid. Statins do have side effects, and changing diet, lifestyle, and exercise can reduce cholesterol for many people.'

'But the pharma companies make millions from statins,' I pointed out.

'They do,' Judy agreed, 'and we have pharmaceutical reps here all the time pushing statins to us. Plus, some of the top doctors in this country have their own research labs in places like Oxford and Cambridge. And do you know who funds those labs?'

I sighed and nodded. 'The pharmaceutical companies.'

'Exactly. There is no doubt that in the past they had tried to discredit Andrew in the press, but I can't believe that they'd actually do something like this. Stuff like that doesn't happen, does it?'

'We're not sure,' I replied. 'I realise that a large drug company having a doctor killed in remote North Wales does seem pretty far-fetched, but we're trying to look at every avenue of enquiry.'

'How well did you know Andrew?' Annie asked.

Judy lowered her eyes before she spoke. 'Erm ... We were colleagues rather than friends,' she said dismissively.

There was something distinctly 'off' about her answer.

'What was he like?' I asked, as I watched carefully for her reaction.

'He was a nice guy,' she said as she rubbed the side of her nose. 'Good at his job. The patients liked him.' Something was making her feel uncomfortable. I immediately wondered about the exact nature of her relationship with Andrew. Were they more than just work colleagues?

'What about outside of being a GP?' I probed again. 'Did he have a partner or was he in any kind of relationship?'

Judy visibly took a breath. 'Not that I know of, but as I said, I didn't know him that well.'

She's definitely hiding something.

'Can you think of anyone who would want to harm him?' Annie asked.

She shook her head as her eyes filled with tears. 'No ... Sorry. I ...'

'You don't need to apologise,' Annie reassured her.

Having stressed that she didn't know Andrew very well, it was strange to see her then dissolve into tears. Maybe it was just the shock of her colleague being murdered. That would upset anyone. But it felt like there was more to it than that.

She blew out her cheeks and then used both hands to wipe the tears from her face. 'It's just been such a shock. That he's gone.'

'Of course,' I said gently.

Annie reached into her pocket, pulled out a small packet of tissues and handed them over to her. 'Here you go.'

'Thank you,' Judy whispered.

Annie shifted in her seat and then asked very gently,

'Can you think of anyone at all who might have wanted to harm Andrew? Any quarrels or arguments?'

'No,' she said, fighting the tremor in her voice. 'As I said, he was a really lovely person.'

I shot a glance over at Annie. My instinct was that Judy's emotional reaction implied that she and Andrew had been more than just colleagues.

'We heard about poor Joseph Reeves,' Annie said in a low voice.

'Yes. That was so incredibly sad.'

'I understand that his father, Tom, blamed Andrew for not diagnosing Joseph sooner? Is that right?' I asked.

'Tom took Joseph's death very hard, as any parent would.'

'And I guess that Joseph's family might have been angry with Andrew for that?' I suggested. I was waiting for Judy to tell us about the incident where Tom Reeves and his brother and sister came to the practice to confront Andrew.

'As far as I was concerned, Andrew did nothing wrong,' Judy said emphatically.

Annie raised an eyebrow. 'We understand that Tom Reeves did come down here about two months ago to confront Andrew?'

'No, that's not quite what happened actually.'

'How do you mean?' I asked.

'It was Tom's sister, Laura, who had come down to confront Andrew. Tom and his brother Ben arrived to calm her down before she did something stupid. She was like a woman possessed. They had to take her away.'

I shot a look over at Annie. Maybe it was Laura Reeves that we now needed to look at?

Judy then made a show of looking at her watch.

Annie and I took that as our cue to leave and started to get up.

'Thank you for your time, Judy,' Annie said kindly.

'No problem,' she reassured us. 'And please let me know if there's anything else I can do to help. I mean it.'

Chapter 14

Annie and I were sitting in the car park at the medical centre trying to get a handle on what Judy Thompson had just told us.

'I guess we need to look at Laura Reeves?' I said, thinking out loud.

'Yes, if she was angry enough to drive down here to confront Andrew, maybe she just took that one step further,' Annie suggested.

'What do we think about the pharmaceutical angle?' I asked.

Annie shrugged. 'Sounds as if the companies making statins were trying to discredit Andrew's research. But there's a long way from employing a PR agency to discredit him in the press, to hiring someone to kill him. For me, it feels far-fetched.'

'You're right. And from what you described, the way that the person shot Andrew and then came over and shot him twice more feels very personal.'

'Yes. That was my instinct anyway. Coffee?'

'You read my mind.' I started the engine and then

grabbed my phone. 'I'm just going to check on how things are at home.'

'How was Rachel when you left this morning?' Annie asked as I dialled Caitlin's phone.

'Much better thanks,' I replied.

'Dad?' Caitlin said as she answered her phone.

'Hi. Just wanted to check in and see how your mum's doing?'

'Fine. We're fine. I've been doing her nails in front of the telly and she seems happy.'

I could tell by the tone of her voice that something wasn't quite right. 'Are you sure?' I asked.

'Yes,' she replied hesitantly. 'It's just that there was a delivery driver up here earlier in a white transit van. He'd got the wrong address. But there was something that wasn't quite right.'

'How do you mean?'

'I don't know. He seemed to be more interested in looking around and asking questions than finding out where the right address was.'

I didn't like the sound of that. 'Where is he now?'

'It's okay. He's gone ... but he had a London accent.'

'You're sure he's gone?' I asked, feeling uneasy.

'Yes. I've been down the track. I took Jack with me.'

'Okay. Just lock all the doors,' I said. 'I'll be back in a bit. Where's the shotgun?'

'I took it out of the cabinet and put it beside the front door.'

'Good. What time does Sam get out of school?' I asked, although I was pretty sure it was 3.30pm on the dot.

'Half three.'

'Right. You stay there with your mother. I'll pick Sam up.'

'Okay. Thanks Dad,' she said, sounding a little more relieved now she'd spoken to me.

'See you in a bit,' I said as I ended the call.

Annie gave me a quizzical look.

'Caitlin said there was a delivery driver up at the farmhouse earlier. She thought he was snooping around. It might be nothing,' I explained, but my instinct was that it wasn't nothing.

'You should get Sam and then get back home.'

I looked at my watch. It was 3pm. 'I've got half an hour before I can pick him up so shall we go for that coffee?'

Chapter 15

Ten minutes later Annie and I were sitting at a table next to the window in the Popty'r Dref café. A young waitress arrived with our coffees. Latte for Annie and a strong black Americano for me.

'Thank you,' I said with a friendly smile.

'Enjoy!' she said as she turned and walked away.

Annie had a curious expression on her face as she watched the waitress go. 'You notice how she didn't give us a second look?'

'How do you mean?'

'I suppose I mean that we look like an old retired couple who have come out for a coffee.'

I smiled. 'I think that's exactly what we are. Not 'a couple' but we look like one.'

'I just feel that when you get to our age you become invisible. As if we're totally irrelevant,' Annie said thoughtfully. 'We're a doddery old couple in the autumn of our lives.'

'Hey, less of the 'doddery',' I joked.

'I'm a retired Crown Court Judge with thirty-five years'

experience of criminal trials, and you were a detective for thirty years. But that doesn't seem to have any value.'

'Yes, I know exactly what you mean. Some people talk to me as if I'm completely incapable. Or make allowances for me as if I've already got dementia.'

Before we could continue our conversation, two uniformed police cars with their sirens and lights – blues and twos – going, sped past and then turned into the side street just across the road from us. Their sirens were so piercing that everyone in the café looked over.

'They're in a hurry,' Annie remarked.

A moment later, they were followed by an ambulance and an unmarked CID car with the lights in its radiator grill flashing.

Something was very wrong.

Instinctively, I stood up as I watched one of the patrol cars manoeuvre to block off the side street directly opposite us.

'Talking of being relevant,' I said, 'we should go and see what's happening. This looks serious.'

Annie stood up and put her coat on.

I took a ten pound note out of my wallet and signalled to the waitress. 'We've got to go,' I said as I put the note down on the table. 'Keep the change.'

Annie and I went outside.

A few concerned onlookers had gathered on the corner of the side street.

We crossed the road and approached.

A young male constable and an older female officer were tying blue and white police tape across the entrance to the street.

The young PC saw me approaching. 'I'm sorry, sir, but we have an ongoing incident so you're not going to be able to use this street I'm afraid.'

'What's going on?' I asked as I looked past him and saw all the emergency vehicles. Blue lights were still flashing outside a house.

'I'm afraid I don't have any details at the moment,' he said as he secured the tape to a lamppost, 'but I am going to have to ask you to clear the area.'

'It's all right, Steve,' the older female officer said as she came over and gave me a smile.

It was Sergeant Tracey White, whom I'd known when she first joined the force twenty years earlier.

'Hello, Frank,' she said with a smile. 'Been a while.'

'Hi Tracey,' I replied. 'Sergeant now?'

She nodded and looked at Steve. 'This is Frank Marshal. He's a bit of a CID legend in these parts.'

'I wouldn't go that far,' I sighed and then pointed down the street. 'What's going on down there?'

'Major incident.'

'And what does that mean?' I asked with a knowing expression.

She signalled for me to move away and then said under her breath, 'There's been a shooting. Paramedics were called out to a house where a pensioner had collapsed. When they arrived, someone came out and shot Sarah three times. From what I've heard, she's not going to make it.'

'Sarah?'

'Sarah Meadows, one of the paramedics.'

'Anyone see anything?'

'Person in a hoodie and mask came out of nowhere and started firing. That's all I know.'

'But they didn't shoot the other paramedic?'

Tracey shook her head. 'No. Sarah's got two children. It's terrible.'

I looked at Annie and then back at Tracey. 'It sounds exactly the same as the Andrew Burrows shooting.'

Tracey nodded and gave me a dark look. 'Yeah, it does.'

'Any idea if it's just a random shooting?'

'No idea, Frank, but it looks like there's some maniac around here shooting people and that's incredibly frightening for everyone.'

Chapter 16

Having picked Sam up from school, I was driving Annie home. We'd only had a few minutes to process the shooting and what we'd discovered about the victim. A lot of what we'd assumed about Andrew Burrows' murder seemed redundant now there was a second victim. However, both he and Sarah Meadows seemed to have been deliberately targeted. Therefore we had to assume that they were linked somehow. Given that one was a GP and the other a paramedic, the link seemed likely to be medical. Had a patient that both Andrew and Sarah had dealings with died under their care? Had they been at all negligent in their treatment or made a mistake? Was there now a relative or friend seeking revenge on both of them? Or was there another explanation that we just hadn't thought of?

'Can we go riding when we get home?' Sam piped up from the back seat of the truck, breaking my train of thought. I looked at him in the rear-view mirror and smiled. 'Yes, mate,' I replied, and watched a broad grin develop across his face.

Annie turned to look at him. 'I take it that you like horse riding then, Sam?'

'Yeah. I love it.'

'He's taken to it like he's been riding all his life,' I said proudly. 'Haven't you mate?'

Sam looked a little awkward at the praise as we pulled up outside Annie's house.

'Here we go,' I said.

'Do you live here on your own?' Sam asked as he gazed at her large house.

'I do,' she said as she opened the passenger door.

'It's a very nice house,' he said thoughtfully.

'Thank you, Sam,' Annie said with an amused smile. 'I'll see you soon.'

'Bye,' he said as he waved to her. I'd noticed that he was really coming out of his shell in recent weeks. It was lovely to watch him grow in confidence.

'Won't be a second, mate,' I said as I got out of the truck. I wanted to have a quick word with Annie before we returned home. And it wasn't a discussion that was appropriate for Sam to hear.

We took a few steps towards her front door.

'I'm assuming the police will have realised that these two shootings can't now be explained as robberies gone wrong,' I said quietly.

She sighed. 'I certainly hope so.'

'I'm just wondering what the link is between Andrew and Sarah,' I said as she fished out her door keys.

'It has to be medical, doesn't it?'

'That's my initial instinct. My guess would be that somewhere along the line, Andrew and Sarah have been involved in an incident where someone has died. Maybe there has been some suggestion of a mistake or negligence, even if it's not been official.'

'And a friend or relative has decided to take revenge on them,' she said, continuing this line of thought. 'I presume that we're now ruling out a connection to Joseph Reeves and his family?'

I shrugged. 'I can't see how Sarah Meadows can be connected to that unless there's something we don't know. But it doesn't sound like the sort of thing that a working paramedic would be involved with.'

'No ... We should talk to Judy Thompson again,' Annie suggested. 'She did say that she would do anything she could to help.'

'I'm wondering if Ethan can access any medical data for us. From Glan Clwyd hospital. We're looking for a patient under the care of Andrew Burrows who was also attended to by Sarah Meadows.'

'I'm going over to see him and Meredith later so I'll ask him.' Annie opened her front door and gestured inside. 'You and Sam are more than welcome to come in for a bit.'

'I'm refusing to come into your house again until you invest in some biscuits,' I joked, 'and I'm pretty sure that Sam will feel the same way.'

'All right, all right,' she said with a laugh. 'I'll get some biscuits just for you two.'

I gave her a smile and our eyes met for a moment. 'Send my regards to Ethan and Meredith, will you?' I said warmly.

Chapter 17

Sam and I drove up the bumpy track towards our farmhouse. Over to our right, thick black clouds had blotted out the silhouettes of the mountains on the horizon. Lightning flickered repeatedly, and then about twenty seconds later came the deep rumble of thunder.

'It's four miles away, Taid,' Sam said as he pointed to rolling black clouds that were heading our way.

'How do you know that?' I asked. I was certain I knew what Sam was going to tell me, but I was intrigued as to how he was going to explain it.

'Light travels much faster than sound. So, you see the lightning but the sound takes longer to get to us,' he reported earnestly.

'Oh right.' I nodded with a half smile as our farmhouse and the annexe came into view.

'And it takes five seconds for the sound of thunder to travel one mile,' he added with a look of great concentration on his face. 'I counted twenty seconds between the lightning and the thunder. So, that's twenty divided by five which is four. So that's four miles.'

I laughed as I pulled the truck over and parked up. 'Wow, that's brilliant!'

He gave me an accusatory frown. 'You must know that, Taid. You've lived out here for a long time.'

'Well, I didn't know,' I said, 'but now I do. So, thanks for explaining it.'

Sam narrowed his eyes as if he wasn't quite sure whether or not to believe me.

As we got out of the truck, Caitlin raced over from the farmhouse with a concerned expression on her face.

My heart sank.

'What's wrong?' I asked anxiously.

'I've lost Mum,' she said frantically.

'What?' I asked. Jack bounded towards us and Sam crouched down to stroke his head.

There was a clap of thunder which made Jack agitated. The storm was getting closer.

Caitlin sighed nervously. 'I'm serious. She was watching the telly. I went out to the kitchen to make us a cup of tea. I came back and she'd vanished.'

'And how long ago was this?' I asked as my pulse started to quicken.

'Ten minutes. Maybe a bit longer,' she said, her voice shaky with anxiety.

'She can't have vanished,' Sam said.

'What about James' room?' I asked as I took a breath. 'She sometimes goes in there and just sits on her own.'

'No.' Caitlin shook her head. 'Seriously Dad, I've looked in every room. She's not in there. I'm so sorry.'

'It's not your fault, love.'

My mind was racing. Where else could she have gone? I had visions of her wandering off into the nearby woods and having a fall. *Jesus.*

'What about the annexe?' I asked.

'No,' she said frantically.

'Okay,' I said in as calm a tone as I could muster. It was important to think rationally and not to panic Caitlin or Sam. 'Don't worry. She can't have gone far.'

All three of us, along with Jack, headed quickly along the track. The sky above us had darkened very quickly and a speck of rain landed on my forehead.

Charging through the front door, I entered the annexe where Caitlin and Sam lived and looked around.

'Rachel? Rachel?' I shouted urgently.

I marched through the living area towards the doors to the two bedrooms.

'Mum?' Caitlin yelled as we all searched the annexe.

'Rachel?' I said as I went into the bathroom and pulled back the shower curtain.

Nothing.

'Nain, are you in here?' Sam called out, joining in.

Making my way back into the living area, I looked at Caitlin.

'No, she's not in here.' My mind now turned to where else she could have gone.

Caitlin looked as if she was on the verge of tears. 'Oh God, I feel so guilty.'

I put my hand on her arm as we all moved outside. 'It's not your fault, love. You were only making a cup of tea.'

It was now teeming down with rain but I didn't care as long as we found Rachel.

'Yeah Mum,' Sam said, taking my lead, 'you only left her for a few minutes.'

There was more thunder, and it was so loud that it seemed to shake the very ground we were standing on.

Caitlin didn't seem to be listening to us. 'Where the hell is she?'

'And you've been through our house thoroughly?' I asked to clarify.

'About three times. Everywhere. Inside wardrobes, behind shower curtains, under the beds, in the pantry. She's not in there, Dad.'

'What about the shed at the back?' I said, but I was already jogging down the wide pathway that went between the farmhouse and annexe.

'It's locked, isn't it?' Caitlin said as she jogged beside me.

The rain was now torrential. Huge drops landed on my eyelashes and I wiped them away as I ran.

'It should be,' I said as the large shed honed into view.

The door was wide open.

The noise of the rain falling was growing in volume by the minute. My hair was now matted to my head.

Jack ran ahead of us, disappeared inside the shed, and barked loudly.

Trying to get my breath, I slowed as I reached the open shed door, fearing what I might find.

Glancing inside, I saw that it was empty.

'She's been here,' I said to Caitlin as I squinted through the rain. My heart was thumping against my chest.

'I don't understand,' Caitlin said. 'Why has she opened the shed?'

I shrugged as I pushed my soaking hair from my forehead.

The black sky suddenly flashed bright with sheet lightning which was immediately accompanied by a crack of thunder.

Then Sam pointed. 'She's over there!' he shouted over the sound of the rain.

Turning around, I saw that Rachel was over by an old flowerbed at the back of the farmhouse.

She was kneeling down on the earth, using a trowel to dig it as if she didn't have a care in the world.

I sighed despondently as we all jogged over towards her. 'Oh God, she must be soaked through.'

'Mum!' Caitlin snapped as we approached.

I put my hand on her arm. 'It's okay. She doesn't understand, does she?'

'What's Nain doing?' Sam asked, looking thoroughly confused.

I went over to Rachel and crouched down beside her. She was digging in a flowerbed where she used to grow vegetables when Caitlin and James were kids. It had been her pride and joy for a long time.

There was another flash of lightning that lit up the sky for a second.

'Hello love,' I said, looking at her cardigan and joggers that were now soaked.

'Oh hello,' she said brightly. Water was splashing off her but she just hadn't noticed.

'You okay, love?' I asked, trying to hide the welling emotion inside. I glanced up at Caitlin and gave her a look to indicate for her and Sam to go back to the annexe out of the storm.

'Just making sure that everything's in order here,' she said, as if she had been transported back to a sunny day twenty years ago. 'I was thinking of putting carrots just here. New potatoes over there. Maybe some garlic too. What do you think?'

She looked up at me with the rain running down her face. I put my hand to her cheek. 'I think that's a great idea. Shall we go in because it's started to rain and we're getting wet,' I suggested gently.

Rachel reached up to her hair and felt that it was wet. 'Oh gosh, I hadn't even noticed.'

I helped her to her feet. 'Here we go,' I said. I took her hand and guided her protectively back towards the farmhouse.

'You know what I fancy, Frank?'

'What's that then?'

'A nice cup of tea.'

I nodded and gave her a smile even though my chest was tight with emotion. 'That's a great idea.'

Chapter 18

Annie was sitting at the table that she'd helped Ethan and Meredith move from the kitchen to the living room. She had then cooked a wonderful 'scouse' stew – even if she did say so herself. Cubes of tender beef, carrots, potatoes, swedes, parsnips, onions, beef stock, splash of red wine, rosemary and thyme.

Ethan patted his stomach. 'That was goat, Annie.' He then kissed his fingers to signal how good the food was.

'It wasn't goat. It was beef. I think goat stew is a Moroccan delicacy.'

Ethan guffawed with laughter.

Annie turned to Meredith, who was wearing a bright orange headscarf over her head to hide the hair loss from her latest course of chemotherapy.

'What's he laughing about?' Annie asked. She got the distinct impression that she'd said something foolish.

Meredith snorted. 'He doesn't mean goat as in billy goat that goes ...' She then did a little impression of the noise a goat makes.

Annie groaned. 'Sorry, I'm completely lost guys. And I feel about a hundred.'

'G.O.A.T.' Ethan said. 'Stands for *greatest of all time*. It's just what people say these days when something or someone is really good.'

'Well, I don't say that,' Annie protested. 'I've never heard of it.'

Meredith shook her head. 'He means young people.'

'Well, that's not very nice,' Annie said with a self-effacing chuckle.

Ethan looked at her with a mischievous grin and teased her with a mock posh accent. 'Gran, that stew was simply delectable.'

Annie chortled, wagging her finger at him. 'Hey, I've warned you about that, buster.'

He gave her a cheeky wink as he got up from the table and collected the plates. 'But seriously. Great food. And it's lovely to have you here,' he said as he headed for the door. 'I've got some work to do so you'll have to excuse me.'

'Anything more on that car?' Annie asked.

He shook his head. 'No, sorry, but I might have something else. Pop in before you go.'

Annie nodded.

Meredith blew out her cheeks and sat back in her seat. 'Well, I'm stuffed.'

'You didn't eat very much.'

'Bloody chemo is affecting my appetite,' she said quietly, and as her face blanched with sorrow she looked away, lost deep in thought.

Silence.

Annie studied her carefully. 'You okay?'

Meredith gave an unconvincing nod and then turned to look directly at her. 'You do know that I'm not getting any better?'

'Don't be silly,' Annie reassured her, but she was aware that the combination of chemotherapy and radiotherapy had not yet worked to rid her of cancer. 'You're not going anywhere.'

Meredith narrowed her eyes. 'I have to face the fact that there is a strong chance that I'm not going to be around in a few years' time.'

'Nonsense,' Annie said a little too sharply. What Meredith was saying was scaring her. 'You can't think like that.'

Meredith sighed. 'I have to be a realist, Mum, and I have to think about Ethan too.'

'Ethan is a very intelligent and capable young man,' Annie said.

'I know that, but he can still be a little naïve at times. I want you to promise me that you'll look out for him.'

Annie reached across the table and took Meredith's hand. 'Ethan is my grandson and I love him very dearly. I'll always look out for him, but I don't want us to be having this conversation.'

Meredith got to her feet. 'Come on then, I'll wash up and you dry.'

'Deal. I've just had my nails done.' Annie stood, noticing that the pain and swelling had almost gone from her knee. Whatever Andrew Burrows had prescribed, it was working. It struck her in that moment that her appointment with him would have been his last. It was so sad.

Watching Meredith stacking the plates, Annie asked, 'Would you like me to buy you a dishwasher?'

Meredith gave her a smile. 'I'd love you to buy me a dishwasher but I haven't got anywhere to put it.'

'Then maybe it's time you moved,' Annie suggested as she passed her another plate.

'We've been in Corwen for years, Mum. Where would we go?'

Annie shrugged. 'I don't know. Closer to me. Somewhere with a bit more space. I've downsized a bit and I have my judge's pension. I know it's indelicate to talk about money, but you and Ethan are my only relatives. I just want to make your lives as comfortable as possible and I have the money to do that. Or you can move in with me. I've got three spare bedrooms.'

Meredith looked a little teary as she spoke. 'Sorry,' she said, wiping her face. 'I just had a thought. What if I'd never decided to find you?'

Annie put the plate down and gave her daughter a tight hug. 'Well, I'm bloody glad you did. And I meant what I said. If you want to move closer to me, I'll get you somewhere with a sodding dishwasher. Or you guys just move in with me. I could do with the company.'

They both smiled.

Chapter 19

Picking up a thick log, I walked over and tossed it onto the fire pit that Caitlin and I were sitting around. The storm had now passed and the night sky was clear above us. For a few seconds, I just stared up at the bright, vanilla-coloured moon. The bowl-shaped craters on its surface seemed particularly pronounced.

After we'd found Rachel, I'd cleaned her up, run her a bath, and found her some clean, dry clothes. She was now fast asleep under a blanket in her armchair with the television on. I couldn't believe that I'd had to resort to locking the front door and the patio doors in case she went walkabout again. I knew that I shouldn't be surprised. I'd had plenty of friends whose wives or husbands had dementia and they'd dealt with exactly the same situation. I guess I was naively hoping that it just wouldn't happen to us.

Caitlin tapped on her phone and the song *Fire and Rain* by *James Taylor* started to play on the Bluetooth speaker that was sitting on a nearby log.

She reached over with her glass of wine and clinked my glass of Jameson's whiskey.

'Cheers, Dad,' she said quietly.

'Cheers,' I replied.

There was a poignant silence between us as we listened to the music.

'Mum used to love James Taylor,' I said softly.

Caitlin looked at me accusingly. 'How do you know she still doesn't?' she asked in a slightly defensive tone.

'Sorry. I didn't mean it like that,' I reassured her. 'I just don't know. And what happened today really scared me.'

Caitlin grimaced. 'I'm so sorry Dad.'

'Hey, I already told you. It wasn't your fault. Your mum's never done anything like that before,' I said calmly, 'but this Lewy Bodies Dementia is a progressive illness. She's only going to get worse, and today was just proof of that.'

Caitlin shook her head sadly and looked intently at the orange flames that danced and flickered in the firepit. For a while, the only sound was the crackle of burning wood.

'We're losing her, aren't we?' she said eventually.

'We are,' I replied in a virtual whisper.

Caitlin took a sip of her wine, then cleared her throat to mask the choke in her voice. 'She's already so different from what she was like when Sam and I first arrived here.'

I gave her an understanding nod. 'I know, love. It sounds like a platitude, but it really is heartbreaking.'

Getting to her feet, she came over to the bench where I was sitting. She took a nearby caramel-coloured blanket, wrapped it around her shoulders, and sat down next to me.

Then she slowly rested her head on my shoulder like she used to do when she was little.

'I feel like she's just fading away in front of us,' she said, her voice trembling with emotion.

Chapter 20

Having tucked Meredith up in bed and kissed her goodbye, Annie went to see Ethan. He was busy typing away and looking intently at the huge double monitor in front of him. The screens were a blur of graphs and rapidly changing numbers. One of them was showing various currency rates along with stock market prices.

'All right there, Gordon Gekko,' Annie quipped.

Ethan frowned as he turned to look at her. 'Gordon who?'

Annie sighed in frustration. 'Gordon Gekko. The film *Wall Street*? Michael Douglas and Charlie Sheen. *Greed is good. Greed works.*'

Ethan laughed as he held up his hands in surrender. 'Woah. You just said a load of stuff but I have no idea what you're talking about.'

Annie sat down next to him. 'I despair of you, Ethan. I really do,' she said in a teasing tone. Then she pointed at the screens. 'What's all this?'

'I'm doing some work for a hedge fund,' he explained.

'Ah, going to the dark side then?' she joked.

'Indeed I am,' he replied, miming lots of money with his fingers.

'Well, remember that money isn't everything,' Annie said, worried that she sounded patronising. 'I don't mean to sound dull or condescending but enjoy the work you do. And if you can, make a difference, help others, and give something back.'

'You sound like, Mum,' he said with a knowing smile.

'It must be genetic then.'

Ethan rubbed his hands over his short beard thoughtfully. 'She's really not well, is she?'

Annie shook her head. 'No she's not, but she's strong. And she's got us to support and look after her.'

'Yes, she has.' Ethan looked genuinely brightened by sharing how he was feeling and hearing her response.

Silence.

Annie then pointed to the bank of computer stuff. 'You said you might have something for us with that car?'

'Oh yes.' Ethan sat up in his chair, swivelled round, and began to tap away. 'I had a thought. Even though the licence plate doesn't actually exist, which means that the killer created it, that fake plate would have been caught on ANPR at some point in the day anyway.'

Automatic Number Plate Recognition – ANPR – was technology that allowed the police to track any vehicle through a computer system that read cars' number plates. These could then be checked against an individual vehicle, or a database of vehicles of interest. There were 20,000 ANPR cameras on traffic lights and along the UK road network and they automatically checked over 90 million licence plates a day.

'Oh yes, of course,' Annie said. 'It's simple when you explain it.'

'So, even though we can't get hold of a registered

owner and address, we can at least track the plate and car on the day of the shooting.'

Annie leaned forward. This could be a significant breakthrough. 'And have you managed to do that?'

'Sort of.' Ethan pointed to a digital map on the screen. 'Our first ANPR hit on the day of the shooting is here. The A487 heading north towards Dolgellau at 7.45am.' He then zoomed in closer, making the digital map bigger. 'The next hit is at 8.09am as the car passes these lights that lead into the Dolgellau Leisure Centre. Weird thing is, the car leaves the centre again at 8.16am so the person only spent seven minutes inside.'

'That is weird, isn't it?' Annie said with a frown as she thought aloud.

Ethan shrugged. 'Maybe they were dropping something off? I don't know. But it's definitely strange to visit somewhere like that only to leave again seven minutes later.'

'Maybe they were picking someone up? Any other hits?'

'Yep,' Ethan nodded and pointed. 'The car arrived at the medical centre at 10.33am.'

'10.33am?' Annie asked to clarify.

'Yes. Which means they stayed there for three hours waiting for Andrew Burrows to leave.'

'That's a long time. But I suppose if they wanted to target him, they'd have to wait for as long as it took for him to leave.'

Ethan gestured to the screen again. 'At 1.36pm, the car leaves the medical centre after the shooting. It then heads north on the A494 to here, Coed y Brenin Park.' He turned to look at Annie. 'And then the car vanishes. There have been no more hits on the ANPR since then.'

Annie took a few seconds to process this. 'Did the killer

drive up there, change the plates back to what they were originally and then drive away?'

'That's one possibility.'

'What's the other possibility?' Annie asked.

'The killer dumped the car up there and switched to a different vehicle. The only problem with that is, without the registration plate, I can't trace anything on the ANPR log.'

Chapter 21

It was 8.30am the following morning by the time Annie and I took the turning to the Dolgellau Leisure Centre. Annie had gained various important bits of information from Ethan last night and we now needed to investigate them fully. I had no idea whether or not the CID team at Dolgellau was investigating along the same lines as us. Frankly, I didn't care. They'd already made a huge blunder when they believed that Andrew Burrows had been killed in a bungled robbery. They were bloody idiots. Or at least DCI Dewi Humphries was. And I certainly wasn't about to hand over what Ethan had discovered to him.

As I parked the car, I glanced down at Jack who was lying fast asleep between us. I'd taken him for a good run at about 6am so he was tired. Then I peered carefully at my phone for any missed calls or messages. Part of me was bracing myself for the next episode involving Rachel at home. But Caitlin was there permanently now and she was looking into whether we could get some kind of allowance for her being her mother's full-time carer. My police pension was very good, but a few more quid would never go amiss.

'Still worried about Rachel?' Annie asked as she turned to look at me.

'Yes, but I have to trust Caitlin. And after yesterday, I think she's going to be extra vigilant. I guess I just worry about where this all ends.'

Annie reached over and touched my arm. 'You know if you need anything, you just have to ask.'

'Thank you,' I said, but I knew that Annie had her own issues with her daughter Meredith.

We got out of the truck, made our way across the wet car park, and went inside the leisure centre.

Over to our right there was a reception desk and a young woman – 20s, blonde, tight ponytail, sporty looking – sitting behind a computer screen chatting and laughing with her young male colleague, who was wearing some very tight sports gear.

We'd already agreed that Annie was going to take the lead. There were still times when I forgot that I couldn't just wander up, flash my warrant card, and start to ask questions. In my head, my age seemed to fluctuate between late 20s and early 30s. But never 70!

'Hi there,' Annie said to the receptionist in a friendly voice. 'Two days ago, I came to the 8am Pilates class.'

'Oh yes,' she said. I hoped that she hadn't spotted Annie's slight limp and realised that she was in no fit state to do a Pilates class at the moment!

'The thing is,' Annie continued, pulling a face, 'someone came out of the car park and banged the wing of my car but they didn't leave a note or anything.'

'Oh no, that's terrible.' The receptionist spoke in a voice that bordered on the patronising tone you might use for a child.

'I've told the insurance company that I'd check to see if there was any CCTV.'

'Erm, okay,' the receptionist said uncertainly as she peered at her screen. 'Let me just have a look.'

I leaned over the desk and spoke to her under my breath. 'We don't really want to get the police involved, but technically that person left the scene of an accident. That is an offence. I should know - I used to be a police officer.'

'Right. Yes.' She seemed a little concerned by my comment, but that was the idea. 'Here we go. What time did you park your car?'

'I was running a bit late,' Annie said. 'I guess it was about 8.05am or just after. There was a silver VW Golf driving quite erratically so I wondered if it could have been that one?'

The receptionist turned her monitor so we could see it. 'And what car were you driving?'

'It's a Land Rover Discovery.'

The screen showed the silver VW Golf driving into the car park at exactly 8.09am as Ethan had told Annie.

Bingo, I thought as I peered at the screen.

I held my breath. The person driving that car was probably responsible for two murders. Were we going to get a clear view of them as they parked and made their way to reception?

'Can you see your car anywhere?' the receptionist asked, now looking confused.

Annie and I were now watching the Golf intently.

However, the car parked directly outside the front of the leisure centre doors.

A figure wearing a black baseball cap got out and made their way inside, but the quality of the image was too poor to see anything more than that.

Bugger.

DEADLY CARE

I pointed at the screen. 'This is the driver who we think hit Annie's car, and that person came in here at 8.09am. Do you have a log of when members come and go?'

'Erm, no. Well, we do on our computer system. It's all done via wristbands. Sorry, I'm confused. I thought you said that this person hit your car in the car park. Where is your car?'

I ignored her question. 'So, if you looked at the computer, you could tell us the name of the member who arrived at 8.09am?'

She looked at us with suspicion. 'Listen, I don't know what's going on here, but if your car isn't in the car park then this person hasn't done anything wrong.' She pointed at the CCTV image that was now paused on her screen. 'I don't know why you want to know who this person is, but I can't tell you that. I'm going to have to ask you to leave the leisure centre please.'

Annie and I glanced at each other in frustration as we turned to go.

Then Annie turned back and looked at the receptionist.

'We think the person driving that car shot Andrew Burrows, the GP who was murdered on Monday. They might also have shot Sarah Meadows, the paramedic who was killed yesterday.'

'What?' The colour visibly drained from the receptionist's face. 'Why aren't the police here checking all this then?'

I raised an eyebrow. 'That's a very good question. The answer is that we don't know, but I worked as a detective for thirty years ...' I gestured to the figure wearing the baseball cap entering the centre, '... and I'm convinced that this person is responsible for two murders.'

The receptionist looked flustered. 'I'm going to need to

talk to my manager about this. I don't have access to the membership log, but if you leave your number I can give you a call about it?'

Annie gave her a grateful smile. 'Thank you.'

Chapter 22

Twenty minutes later, Annie and I arrived at the Coed y Brenin Park – it was Welsh for *the King's forest*. Covering 9,000 acres, the park was famous for its popular mountain bike trails and hiking routes.

As we drove into the forest, we followed the signs to the main car park. The only information we had was that the silver VW Golf had turned into Coed y Brenin Park but hadn't been spotted on the ANPR cameras after that.

The sun slanted down through the trees, making dappled patterns on my windscreen and the road. There was a diverse mix of broadleaf and conifer trees, but the most prominent and impressive were the towering Douglas Firs, known as 'The King's Guards'. Several of them stretched up to over 150 feet.

We parked and got out. It was a weekday, so the only visitors seemed to be people 'of a certain age' who had come for a walk and a cup of tea in one of the cafés.

'You think the killer switched cars?' Annie asked.

'Either that or they replaced the original number plates, but my instinct is that it's highly suspicious to be switching around number plates out in the open. My guess is that they had another car parked up here.'

We looked around the large car park but there was no sign of the silver Golf.

I had an idea.

Over to our right there was a one-storey wooden building that housed an information centre.

'Come on,' I said with a nod towards it.

'What are we doing?'

'Just trust me and go with it.'

Annie gave me a withering look. 'Well don't march off without me. I'm still walking wounded, remember?'

'Yes. Sorry.' I waited patiently for her to catch up. We walked for a few more seconds until we arrived at the door. Then I turned to Annie. 'Are you okay to have mild dementia for the next ten minutes?' I asked.

'Jesus, Frank.' She gave a little groan. 'I have no idea what you're up to, but yes, no problem.'

We walked inside.

Over to our right was an information desk with maps, leaflets etc. Up on the wall was a coloured map of the park and forest showing mountain bike trails and suggested walks, all marked with brightly coloured dots.

A rotund bearded man in his 40s was sitting behind the desk looking at a computer screen and using a mouse.

I nudged Annie and gestured to a shelf of souvenirs which was to the left of us. 'Stay here for a second,' I whispered, 'and look a bit confused.'

She gave me a forced and very sarcastic smile. 'Oh yes. No problem. I can definitely do confused.'

I wandered over to the desk and caught the eye of the man behind the counter.

'Hi there,' I said in a low voice.

'Hi, how can I help?' he asked with a friendly smile.

I leaned forward over the desk a little. 'Listen, this is a bit embarrassing, but I wonder if you can help?' Then I pointed over to Annie. 'My wife has the early stages of dementia.'

He gave me an empathetic look. 'Oh no. I'm sorry to hear that.'

'Thank you. Thing is, on Monday morning she jumped in her car and drove up here to go for a walk without telling anyone. Then she got completely lost, rang me, and I had to drive up to find her.' Then I pulled a face. 'Thing is, she can't remember where she parked her car. I've driven round all the car parks but I just can't see it.'

The man nodded thoughtfully. 'Right …'

'I wondered if any cars had been left here overnight since Monday without parking tickets? I assume that you guys would notice something like that. I just don't want to make a fuss as she's very embarrassed about the whole thing,' I said very quietly.

'Of course,' he said gently under his breath. 'I completely understand. Could you tell me the make and model of your wife's car?'

'Yes,' I replied. 'It's a silver VW Golf.'

His expression changed immediately. 'Oh gosh. Erm …'

'Do you know where it is?' I asked. He clearly knew something about the car but I couldn't work out what the problem was.

'I'm not sure how to tell you this,' he said apologetically, 'but we found a burned out silver VW Golf in the middle of the woods on Monday afternoon. I'm really sorry.'

'Oh dear. Well, it's not your fault,' I reassured him. 'Any idea what happened?'

He shook his head. 'No. I'm so sorry.'

'Did you call the police?' I asked.

'Yes, but they weren't interested.' He shrugged. 'They said they've had a spate of teenagers stealing cars and then torching them. They did say they'd send a patrol car to have a look but we're still waiting.'

I couldn't believe what I was hearing. The lack of joined-up thinking was startling.

'Could you show me on that map where the car is?' I asked. 'I'm going to need to take some photos for the insurance company.'

'Of course.' He turned around to the map and placed his forefinger on part of the forest that looked like it was no more than a five-minute drive away. 'Just here.'

'Thank you.' Then I frowned. 'And you didn't see anything suspicious on Monday? Anyone acting strangely, or anything out of the ordinary?'

'Gosh, you sound like a policeman.'

'I used to be,' I admitted. 'Thirty years as a detective inspector actually.' I thought I'd lay it on thick so that he might now trust me and inform me of anything that had seemed out of place.

He looked almost thrilled as he leaned closer. 'Actually, I did notice a woman acting very strangely that day. She ran into the car park looking flustered, and she kept looking behind her. It was very strange, now that I think about it.'

'Can you tell me what time that was roughly?'

'Just after lunchtime. Around 2.00pm.'

That fits exactly with the timeframe that we're working with, I thought.

'That's brilliant. Thank you.' I spotted the man's delight at my compliment. 'Do you think you could describe her?'

He nodded eagerly. 'I guess she was in her late 30s.

Nicely dressed. And she had very red hair. And I mean very.'

'Do you mean she had dyed hair?'

He shook his head. 'Oh no. I mean she was very ginger. And it was curly.'

That sounds very much like Carol Reeves.

'That wasn't the only weird thing,' he added.

'Go on,' I encouraged him.

'She then jumped in a car and sped out of the car park like the clappers. It was really dangerous. She actually clipped one of our fences on the way out.'

'I don't suppose you got a look at the car or the registration plate?' I asked hopefully.

'It was quite a long way away,' he said, 'but it was definitely a BMW. And it was a dark colour. Navy or black I think.'

I gave him a grateful nod. 'That's great. Thanks for your help.'

Chapter 23

Annie, Jack and I got out of the truck where I'd parked it off the road in the middle of the forest. Jack trotted away and then circled back towards us.

'You think it was Carol Reeves who he saw up here?' Annie asked. I'd just recounted what the man in the information centre had told me.

'Curly red hair, well dressed, in her 30s,' I said. 'It sounds like her.'

'We know why she might want to shoot Andrew Burrows,' Annie said, 'but what's her link to Sarah Meadows?'

'No idea, but it has to be worth looking at.'

She nodded in agreement as we stared at the blackened wreck of the Golf that sat in a small clearing about thirty yards from the road. The air still carried the thick smell of burned metal and rubber. Jack was scurrying around the undergrowth and sniffing the air.

I reached into my toolbox and grabbed a hefty crowbar. 'Right, let's see if there's anything left inside. I'm hoping we can get the VIN number.'

The Vehicle Identification Number – VIN – was a unique 17-character code that identified a specific vehicle. It was usually stamped into the chassis and the engine. A VIN was more reliable than a number plate as it was essentially a unique 'fingerprint'.

We went around the bonnet which had been charred black and brown by the fire. Then I went to the driver's door. It was incredibly stiff where the metal had warped and twisted. Pushing the crowbar into the hinge, I managed to get it open. The metal creaked and crunched as the door moved. Then I reached into the footwell under the steering wheel and popped the catch on the bonnet.

'Smart move to torch the car,' Annie said as I came back round. I reached under the bonnet and eventually managed to lift it. 'There won't be any forensics left.'

Putting on gloves, I searched the engine looking for where the VIN might have been stamped. I swept the black soot from the engine block and saw what I was looking for.

'Bingo,' I said as I reached for my camera and took a photo of the VIN. 'The DVLA will have a record of this number and the registered owner.'

Annie raised her eyebrows. 'And how are we going to get that then?'

We looked at each other and then said in unison, 'Ethan.'

I went around to the side of the car, forced opened the rear door behind the driver's seat, and checked to see if there was anything inside the car.

Annie did the same on the opposite side.

'Anything?' I asked.

She shook her head. 'No,' she said, sounding a little frustrated.

'I'll try the boot.'

'Hold on a second …' She had spotted something.

She leaned in, put her hand under the passenger seat, and retrieved a small object. She held it up to show me. It was a small pair of scissors that had been blackened by the fire, but because they were made from steel they were intact.

I shrugged. A small pair of scissors wasn't much use to us.

'You know what these are, don't you?' she said with a knowing expression.

I scratched my chin in feigned confusion. 'I'm pretty sure they're a pair of scissors.'

She gave me an ironic smile. 'Okay there Mr Sarcastic Pants … They also happen to be left-handed scissors. Stephen was left-handed so we had pairs of these at home.'

I took a moment to process this, then I gave Annie a quizzical look. 'What about the shooting?'

'Sorry?'

I wondered if we'd actually stumbled upon something significant. 'What hand did the killer shoot the gun with?'

'Oh my God.' Annie's eyes widened. 'They were holding the gun in their left hand. Why didn't I think of that before?'

'Well, I'm glad you've thought of it now. It might prove very useful,' I said as I went around to the boot. I clicked the release and lifted up the hatchback. I searched through the charred remains of whatever had been inside the boot but there was nothing there of any significance.

Out of the corner of my eye, I saw a navy Astra and a marked police car stop on the road and then park behind my truck.

'Uh oh,' Annie said as she followed my gaze.

'This is going to go down well,' I said with an expression of faint amusement. I was pretty sure I recognised the

Astra as the one that Dewi and Kelly drove. If I'd pissed them off by getting to the Golf before they did, then I was happy.

A few seconds later, Dewi, Kelly, Ian and two uniformed officers walked up the pathway through the trees to where we were standing.

Dewi had a face like thunder as he glared at me. I had to admit that I did enjoy seeing him annoyed, especially when I'd got one over on him. It might have been petty, but he was a first-class prick.

He glared at me. 'What the fuck are you two doing here?' he asked angrily.

I smirked. 'Having a picnic. What does it look like?'

'It looks like you're trespassing on a crime scene,' he snarled.

I ignored him and looked over at Kelly and Ian. 'Hi Kelly. Ian. We've had a quick look but we couldn't find anything.' I wasn't about to tell them about the scissors quite yet.

'Thank you, Frank,' Kelly said calmly. 'I'll have a look just to double check.'

I looked at Dewi and could see the cogs in his little brain whirring away. I was surprised there wasn't smoke coming out of his ears.

Then he fixed me with an unblinking stare. 'How the hell did you find the car here?'

I tapped the side of my nose. 'Basic detective work, Dewi.'

I could almost feel him bristle with anger. 'If I find that you two clowns have been hacking into our ANPR system, I'll arrest you for perverting the course of justice.'

'Yeah, okay,' I snorted derisively.

Annie took a step towards Dewi. 'I assume after the incident yesterday that you're no longer treating these shootings as robberies that have gone wrong or got out of hand?'

His nostrils flared. 'I'm not going to divulge the nature of an ongoing investigation to you two.'

I signalled to Annie that we should go. 'I'll leave you to it then, Dewi,' I said with a look of amusement that was intended to wind him up.

'Stay out of my fucking way, Frank,' he growled. 'I'm warning you.'

A flash of irritation pulsed through me. The absurdity of this petty little man running a CID team made me angry.

'I'm pretty sure you told me that when you messed up the Marcus Daniels' investigation,' I said.

'And the investigation into my sister's murder,' Annie added forcibly.

Dewi blanked both of us. He took out his blue forensic gloves, pulled them on, and then headed for the car.

Kelly glanced at me. Her look suggested she didn't think that Annie or I were a million miles away from the truth. It was a shame that she wasn't running the Dolgellau CID team.

Ian came towards me with a bemused look on his face and whispered under his breath, 'From what I can see, it's a pity that you're not running this investigation, Frank. The only bright note is that our DCI is finally off to the IOPC tomorrow for a few days.'

'That is a bright note,' I agreed. I saw Dewi looking over suspiciously, clearly wondering what we were talking about.

'See you later, Frank,' Ian said with a nod.

'See you,' I replied. I hoped that Ian stuck around at Dolgellau CID.

Annie and I turned away and headed back to my truck.

Chapter 24

Annie and I were sitting opposite Judy Thompson in her consulting room. Her face was a picture of confusion.

'I'm at a loss for words,' she admitted. 'This sort of thing just doesn't happen in Dolgellau, does it? I watched the BBC's Breakfast News and it was the main breaking story.'

'I've never known anything like this and I was born and bred around here,' I said.

Annie sat forward on her chair. 'Judy, did you know Sarah Meadows?'

'Not really,' she replied. 'Only to say hello to. But I've been their family doctor for a while.'

There was the slightest hesitation as she spoke. This suggested that there was something more to this than she was telling us.

'What kind of family are they?' I asked nonchalantly.

'Troubled, I'm afraid. Sarah's brother, Kevin, has had issues with drugs and addiction. And I know that he's known to the police here.'

I wondered if that had anything to do with what had

happened to Sarah. The name Kevin Meadows didn't ring a bell with me but it had been a long time since I'd been a police officer in the area.

'Undoubtedly, these two shootings weren't anything to do with a robbery,' Annie stated.

'No,' Judy agreed, 'that is obvious now. It makes it all the more frightening for everyone who lives here.'

'It's clear that the person who shot Andrew also shot Sarah,' Annie added.

'Yes. The police were back here this morning but they wouldn't tell me anything. Do you have any suspicions?'

'Not really,' I said, 'that's why we've come to talk to you again. The first thing we'd like to do is see if we can look at the CCTV footage of the car park and the shooting.'

Judy paused in thought. 'I know that the police have that video but I don't know if Suzie made them a copy or sent over the actual file.'

Annie turned to me. 'Suzie is one of the lovely receptionists who works here.'

'You can ask her on your way out,' Judy said, then turned to her computer and typed quickly. 'I'm just sending her a quick message to tell her that we're helping you and that it's fine for her to show you that CCTV.'

'Thank you,' I said.

'We think you might be able to help us with both shootings,' Annie chimed in.

'Really? Isn't this a matter for the police?'

I rubbed my beard and sighed. 'I'm not sure how much we trust the local police to do a proper investigation. Annie and I have had several encounters with them in the past year in which they have been completely incompetent.'

Judy gave a slow nod of realisation and looked at Annie. 'That's right, I remember Andrew telling me about your poor sister. And of course I read about it too. I'm so sorry. That must have been devastating.'

'It was,' Annie admitted, 'and it still is.'

'Understandably so,' Judy said with an empathetic expression. 'You poor thing.'

'The local police and CID were inept and careless at the time and I've never forgiven them for that,' Annie said, visibly taking a breath, 'which is why Frank and I are looking into this ourselves.'

'And why do you think that I might be able to help you?' Judy asked as she crossed her legs and looked at us intently.

'There has to be something that links both Andrew and Sarah,' I explained. 'Given that they were a GP and a paramedic, the logical conclusion is that the connection is a medical one.'

Annie pushed a stray strand of hair from her face and looped it behind her ear. 'We think that Andrew and Sarah must both have been involved in a recent case where something went terribly wrong.'

'Yes, that does make sense,' Judy acknowledged. 'I'm just trying to think.'

I remembered the description that the man at the information desk had given of the woman in Coed y Brenin Park and narrowed my eyes. 'Do you know if there's any connection between Carol Reeves, the mother of Joseph Reeves, and Sarah Meadows?'

Judy raised an eyebrow. 'Carol Reeves?'

'Yes, earlier today we were given a description of someone that might have fitted Carol Reeves in relation to something. It's just a line of enquiry that we're looking at.'

'Not that I can think of,' Judy said. 'Sarah was a paramedic and Joseph was sick with leukaemia. I can't think of a reason why their paths would cross.'

'No,' Annie agreed. 'It doesn't seem likely.'

'Anything else you can think of?' I asked.

She shook her head, but then her expression changed as something occurred to her.

'What is it?' I encouraged her.

She held up her hand as she turned her chair back to the computer and started to type. 'Something happened about two or three months ago. Andrew was called to a house just outside Dolgellau. A woman in her 60s had had a heart attack. I can't remember her name. Police officers had found her and called the paramedics. One of the paramedics had verified her death. We refer to it as PLE – Pronouncing Life Extinct. But, as you might already know, only a registered doctor can complete the Certificate of Death, which Andrew did when he got there.'

'What happened?'

'The woman was taken to Glan Clwyd mortuary for a post-mortem. She was suffering from something called *Lazarus Syndrome*?'

Annie shook her head. 'I've never heard of it.'

'It's pretty rare. There's about a hundred cases a year in the UK. The use of CPR can cause a problem with getting the heart started again. Sometimes the pressure used can trap air in the lungs, which causes pressure on the ribcage and the heart. And that prevents the heart from restarting. However, on these very rare occasions the air clears, the pressure drops, and the heart starts to beat again. The person is unconscious, so nobody is aware that they have essentially come back to life.'

I raised my eyebrows in surprise. 'No, I've never heard of it either.'

'Of course,' Annie nodded. 'Jesus brought Lazarus back to life after four days. Gospel of John, I think.'

I gave her a quizzical look. I didn't know that she had such an in-depth knowledge of the Bible.

'So, what happened?' I asked, trying to work out the relevance.

Judy pointed to her screen. 'I've got it here in our records. Tuesday 10th January. Tina Lott. After a while the chief pathologist realised that she was still alive while in the mortuary. He called the crash team and she was rushed to the ICU, but she fell into a coma and died the following day.'

'And the family blamed Andrew and the paramedic for pronouncing her dead?' Annie asked.

Judy peered at the screen and read the notes. 'That's right. There are some details on here about the family pursuing a legal case of medical negligence. But, as I said, this is a medical condition.'

'Can you see if Sarah Meadows was an attending paramedic on that day?' I asked.

Judy began to type again. After a few seconds, she turned and looked at us in alarm. 'Yes. Sarah was one of the attending paramedics.'

Annie and I glanced at each other. Now we had our link between Andrew Burrows and Sarah Meadows.

FIVE MINUTES LATER, Annie and I were sitting behind the reception area of the medical centre with Suzie. She was using her mouse to locate the CCTV footage from Monday.

'I sent it over as a file to a DC Kelly Taylor,' she explained.

'Yes, we know Kelly,' I said.

She looked a little confused. 'Is there anything else you want to see or just the video?'

I didn't blame Suzie for being nosey. After all, she must have wondered why two people in their 70s were so interested in something like this.

Annie gave her a kind smile. 'We just want to see the video if that's all right?'

'Oh yes, of course,' she said with a forced laugh as she clicked on the MP4 file and it opened up on the screen.

Then she pressed play, and I could see the car park from the cameras that were mounted high above the main reception doors.

Suzie took a breath. She looked upset. 'If you don't mind,' she said quietly, 'I'm going to leave you to it. I don't really want to watch this again. It's very upsetting.'

Annie gave her an empathetic nod. 'Of course, I completely understand.'

Suzie went to the rear of the reception area while Annie and I watched the video.

After a few seconds, Dr Andrew Burrows came marching out of the main doors and headed over to his car on the right of the screen.

Then Annie came out and walked slowly to her Land Rover Discovery on the left of the screen.

Andrew took his mobile phone from his jacket pocket and started to have an animated conversation as he put his briefcase down on the bonnet of the car.

'I see what you mean,' I said to Annie as we watched. 'He does look a bit jumpy.'

'I just wish I'd heard what he was talking about on the phone,' she said.

Apart from Annie and Andrew, the car park was deserted of people.

After a few more seconds, a hooded figure appeared at

the bottom right of the screen. They strode towards Andrew and then stopped.

Then they held up the handgun in their left hand and shot him.

Andrew clasped at his chest and collapsed to the floor.

The figure walked purposefully towards where he was lying, looked down at him, and then shot him twice more from close range.

Then they leaned down, took Andrew's wallet from his jacket, grabbed the briefcase from the bonnet of the car, turned back and walked away.

I glanced at Annie. 'Well now we know that the shooter is definitely left-handed.'

Chapter 25

As Annie and I walked down the windowless corridor towards the morgue at Glan Clwyd Hospital, the drop in temperature was noticeable. Annie had attempted to do some digging around in Tina Lott's family but had pretty much drawn a blank. It seemed that the Lott family owned a farm about ten miles outside Dolgellau.

We arrived at the black double doors that led into the mortuary. I glanced over at Annie.

'I know that you've been back here since you saw Meg,' I said, referring to her late sister, 'but if it's going to be upsetting going in here ...'

She shook her head and then reached out and touched my arm. 'That's very thoughtful of you, Frank, but I'll be fine. I'm determined to find out who killed Andrew and that's keeping me focussed.'

We made our way inside and the air felt immediately icy. Two large examination tables were nearby, with a third on the far side of the room. The walls were tiled to about head height in pale celeste tiles, and some work benches

DEADLY CARE

and an assortment of luminous coloured chemicals ran the full length of the room.

Glancing around, I spotted Professor Gareth Fillery – late 60s, tall, greying hair – over by a body on a metal gurney. I'd known Gareth for many years and he'd been very helpful and sensitive when dealing with Annie's sister, Meg, when she was murdered six months ago. He was dressed in pale blue scrubs, blue latex gloves, and a fetching red bandana with a Wrexham FC badge at its centre.

He spotted us, gave us a friendly smile and a wave, and came bowling over.

'Up the town,' I said, pointing to his Wrexham FC bandana.

'It's looking like promotion into the Football League, Frank,' he said brightly.

I sighed and smiled at him. 'I know. Everything's changed since those American fellas took over.'

Gareth shrugged. 'Hey, if it gets us out of the bloody National League I'm not complaining. The town could do with a bit of a lift for a change.'

'You're not wrong,' I agreed.

'You ever get up to the racecourse?' he asked.

I shook my head. 'Not for a couple of years.'

'You've got your grandson living with you, haven't you?'

'Yes. Sam.'

'My nephew is the team's physio so I can get tickets. Why don't you and Sam come and see a game sometime?' he suggested.

'Yes. I think he'd love that,' I said with a grin.

He gave me a reassuring wink. 'Great stuff. Now, how can I help you guys?'

Annie looked at him. 'Do you remember Tina Lott?'

Gareth's expression changed and his eyes widened. 'Bloody hell. Yes ... I don't think I'm ever going to forget that poor woman.'

'Lazarus Syndrome?' I asked.

'Aye. I'd heard about it but never thought it would happen to me here.'

Annie raised an eyebrow. 'Can you tell us what happened?'

He pointed over to a steel gurney. 'I had her there a few months ago. Suspected cardiac arrest. I'd even marked her up and started the electronic sternal saw when her bloody eyes flickered open a little. I completely shat myself.' He glanced at Annie. 'Excuse my French.'

'Don't worry,' she reassured him, 'I think I would have shat myself too in the same situation.'

'I checked her pulse and realised that she was alive,' Gareth went on, 'so I rang the ICU and they sent down a crash team.' He let out an exaggerated sigh. 'Never experienced anything like it.'

'We heard that she didn't make it,' I said in a sombre tone.

'That's right. She'd been here for hours before I realised that she was alive. I guess it was too late by then.'

'Did you meet her family?' Annie asked.

'Yes. I felt it was only proper that I be around to explain what had happened and give them as much information as possible.'

'At the risk of asking a silly question ...' Annie said, '... how did they seem?'

'Very upset. And angry. I mean she was only 62 years old. That's no age these days, is it?'

'No,' I agreed.

Gareth gave me a questioning look. 'What's your interest in this?'

'We think her death might be linked to the two shootings we had over in Dolgellau,' I explained. I'd known Gareth long enough to trust him to be discreet with what I told him.

'Yeah, I saw that. All over the television.' He looked confused. 'I can't see how this is connected?'

'The two victims were Andrew Burrows and Sarah Meadows,' Annie explained. 'They were the paramedic and doctor who pronounced Tina Lotts dead.'

Gareth puffed out his cheeks as he processed what Annie had told him. 'Right. Christ. You think that someone from Tina's family has some kind of grudge against them?'

'Looks like that,' I replied. 'It's the only connection that we can find.'

'Blimey,' he said. 'It wasn't their fault. Tina Lotts was medically dead when they examined her.'

Annie shrugged. 'Some people don't see it like that. And they need to blame someone.'

'What did you think about the family?' I asked.

Gareth narrowed his eyes. 'You mean, do I think that any of them are capable of doing that kind of thing?'

'Not in so many words,' I said, 'but did any of them seem particularly angry?'

He thought about this for a few seconds. Then he gave us a dark look and nodded. 'Yes. The daughter. Beccy, I think her name was. She lost it. Ranting and raving. She was going to sue the hospital and the doctor. If you're looking for someone to have done this, I'd look at her. Strictly off the record.'

'Of course,' I reassured him as I glanced at Annie. We had a new suspect.

Chapter 26

Annie and I had managed to track down Beccy Lott via a couple of local press articles. She owned *The Coffee Pot*, a relatively new café in Dolgellau and one which neither I nor Annie had visited.

As we sat down at a corner table, I looked around the modern, tasteful interior. The menu of coffees, teas, and breakfasts was written neatly on a chalkboard. The *Smashed Avocado on Sourdough* told me everything I needed to know.

'Not a bloody sausage in sight,' I groaned as I pointed to the breakfast menu on the wall.

Annie laughed. 'Not these days. You'll be lucky to find bacon. Processed meats are very bad for you.'

'Yes, but they taste fantastic,' I chortled.

'I'm not going to disagree with you there,' Annie said as she put on her glasses.

I looked around and frowned. 'What did this place used to be?'

'When I was a child, it was a toy shop. My mother used to bring me past here on the way to the butchers and the greengrocers. And I know it sounds like a cliché, but I really did push my face up against the window to look at all the toys.' Annie was now momentarily lost in her childhood memory. 'This was before Meg was born. There were these beautiful dolls in the window. Sweet Rosemary. That's what they were called. Very elegant. The one I wanted had these little dangly drop earrings, fake pearl necklace, and a beautiful ivory-coloured silk dress. Her hair was all done up as if she was going to a ball, and she had dark hair and blue eyes like my mother. I wanted that doll so desperately. As if my life would be complete if I could take her home with me?'

'And did you?'

Annie shook her head with a slight look of sadness. 'No. My mother said it was too expensive. I think it was ten shillings.'

'I wonder if this was the same place where I bought a box of 'Army Men' figures,' I said, happy to join in with the reminiscing. 'In those days they were made from metal, and you could buy these tiny pots of colour to paint their uniforms on. They changed them to plastic a few years later. It wasn't quite the same.'

'I think that's because they used to make toys from lead, and then everyone panicked about children getting lead poisoning.'

'Probably,' I said, but I was still remembering setting up banks of toy soldiers on the carpet. I'd put them in rows, with their guns facing the door to my bedroom just in case anyone came in. I felt secure in the knowledge that if any intruder did come in, my trusty 'Army Men' would blast them to smithereens.

A young waitress – early 20s, black hair, pale face – came over and handed us two menus, breaking my train of thought.

'Here you go,' she said with a distracted smile. 'I'll be

back in a minute to take your order.'

'Is Beccy around?' I asked her, getting my head back into detective mode.

'No, sorry. She's not in today I'm afraid.'

'This is her café, isn't it?' Annie asked to clarify.

'Yes, that's right,' the girl nodded awkwardly.

'We popped in yesterday morning to see her,' I explained, now probing to see if Beccy had been in the café at the time of Sarah Meadows' shooting.

'She's had a couple of days off,' the waitress said. 'Do you want me to pass on a message or anything?'

'No, it's fine. Just wanted to say hello that's all.'

'Oh, okay then,' she said with a shrug as she wandered back to the counter.

Annie was looking past my shoulder at something on the wall behind my head. I turned back to look.

There were photos of a woman in her 30s. One of them showed her in hospital with a scarf over her head. I assumed that she'd been having some kind of chemotherapy for cancer. The other photos showed her running a marathon, skydiving, and abseiling – clearly events designed to raise money for a cancer charity. There was also a newspaper article which showed a photo of her with a large cheque, and the caption – *Brave Beccy Lott has raised an astonishing £14,500 for Cancer Research in the past year.*

I felt a slight pang of guilt as I looked back at Annie. But then I reminded myself that this was the woman who we suspected might be responsible for gunning down two innocent people in Dolgellau in the space of a few days.

'Could that be her?' I asked Annie.

She shrugged. 'Hard to tell from a photograph.'

'Looks like Beccy has had a rough time of it,' I said, pulling a face.

Annie gave me a look. 'Doesn't mean she didn't do

this.' She gestured to the photos behind me. 'In fact, given what she's been through, losing her mother like that might have been the straw that broke the camel's back.'

'We probably need to engineer a way of talking to her,' I suggested.

Annie got up gingerly from the table. 'Leave it to me.'

'What are you doing?' I asked.

She tapped her nose and smiled.

The waitress came wandering back over. 'Have you had chance to think about what you'd like?'

'Actually, dear,' Annie said, 'we're rather at a loss. Frank and I have been raising money for Beccy's charity. She knows all about it.' She tapped her coat pocket. 'I've got a rather sizeable cheque here to give her. I'd like to give it to her personally which is why we came in here. If you could tell us where she lives, then Frank and I could pop over and give it to her directly. We're off on holiday tomorrow you see and I'd like to give it to her before we go away.'

The waitress took a long breath. 'Erm … I don't … I'm not really sure I can give you Beccy's address.'

Annie gave a little chortle of laughter and touched the waitress's arm. 'Do Frank and I really look like a pair of vicious burglars, dear? And you look like a very sensible young lady to me. We'd be so grateful if you could help us out.'

The waitress thought for a few seconds.

I stood up and raised my hand. 'It's okay. Please don't worry,' I said in a friendly voice. 'We shouldn't have asked you. We'll be on our way.'

She looked at us as we got our things together. 'It's okay. Sorry. I'll scribble down Beccy's address for you.'

Annie gave her a grateful look. 'Aw, that's so incredibly kind of you, dear.'

Chapter 27

As we pulled out of Dolgellau, Annie typed Beccy Lott's address into my Sat Nav. Jack was sitting upright beside us looking out of the window, his tongue lolling a little.

'Thatta boy,' I said as I scruffed the top of his head. 'Come on, lie down.'

Jack lay down on the bench seat between me and Annie.

Annie pointed at the digital map on my dashboard. 'Okay, less than ten minutes. What did we do before these Sat Nav things?'

'Used a map? And our common sense?' I joked.

'Yeah, all right smart arse,' she groaned. 'No doubt you can find your way around Snowdonia by the position of the sun.'

I shrugged and gave her a faint smile. 'Of course. And I can tell the time by the month we're in and the position of the sun.'

'The Welsh Crocodile Dundee,' Annie said sceptically as she reached over and covered the clock on the Ford

Ranger's dashboard. 'Go on then, Mr Man of the Wilderness.'

I smiled as I peered out of the windscreen and then up at the sun that was partially covered by cloud. Then I gave Annie my best thoughtful expression as I glanced surreptitiously at the watch on my right wrist which was partially covered by my sleeve. Unlike most people, I favoured my right wrist for my watch, and had done since being a police officer. It was my dominant hand when I was writing in my notebook, using my radio, and even driving. These were moments when I often needed to check the time quickly, so to me it made more sense for it to be on the right.

The dial of my watch peeked from under my jacket sleeve. It was 2.30pm.

'Definitely between 2pm and 3pm,' I said, trying not to smirk. 'Hard to tell with all the cloud, but if I had to guess I'd say about 2.30pm.'

Annie took her hand from the clock on the dashboard to see that it was 2.30pm. Then she gave me a very suspicious look. 'I've no idea how you did that, but I know it wasn't the alignment of the sun in the sky.'

I grinned and then gave a laugh. 'I told you. I've lived in the country all my life, Annie. Grew up on a farm. You wouldn't understand.'

She huffed with mock indignation. 'Don't you patronise me, Frank Marshal.' Then she reached over and pulled the sleeve over my left wrist back to reveal there was no watch.

I allowed a few seconds before I laughed, then lifted up my right arm to show her my watch.

'You bugger!' she chuckled.

I watched her for just a second. She had what I called 'a fruity chuckle', and her whole face and eyes lit up as she laughed.

Then I flicked my eyes up to the rear-view mirror.

There had been an old, dark green Land Rover Defender behind us for several miles, taking the same turnings as we had.

It was now sitting about twenty yards behind us but getting closer.

'Everything okay?' Annie asked, noticing my distraction.

'I'm not sure.' I kept my eyes fixed firmly on the rear-view mirror while glancing ahead occasionally.

Annie shuffled down in her seat to look in the wing mirror.

'The Land Rover?' she asked.

'Yes. It's been behind us for quite a while. I think it's following us.'

Annie turned to me. 'Well, you're not easily spooked so there must be something wrong. Can you see the driver?'

'No, just a figure.'

'Licence plate?' she asked, as she took out her phone.

'Yes,' I said as I squinted to see the registration in the vibrating mirror. 'Erm, Yankee, Foxtrot, One, One, Zebra, Whiskey, Tango.'

She typed the number into her phone. 'I'll ping it over to Ethan to see if he can find anything.'

'Okay,' I said. 'I'm just going to make sure we're being followed, so hold on.'

Annie gripped the sides of her seat.

Jack sat up and gave a little whine. He could sense my growing agitation.

Spotting a side road to our right, I checked the Land Rover.

Then, without warning or hitting the brakes, I spun the wheel right and we careered off the main road and down a small residential side road.

The tyres squealed with the force of the turn.

Glancing anxiously up at the rear-view mirror, I saw that the Land Rover was still following us.

'Bollocks,' I muttered under my breath.

Annie turned back to look. She was starting to get concerned. 'Who the hell is going to be following us?' she asked.

'I'm guessing it's someone who doesn't want us poking our noses into the shootings.'

She thought for a second. 'Who would know that we're snooping around?'

'I've no idea, but I can't think of any other reason, can you?'

'Not really,' she said quietly.

There was the growl of an engine as the Land Rover came roaring up behind us.

Up ahead, the road was narrow with houses and parked cars on both sides of the road.

We were now travelling at 60mph, which made weaving in and out of the cars increasingly dangerous.

Over to my right, there were children on the pavement playing on bikes. I just prayed that one of them didn't pull out in front of us.

We reached the end of the housing, and the road opened up so that there were just fields either side.

With a look in the wing mirror, I saw that the Land Rover had now pulled out and was travelling on the other side of the road.

'What is this clown doing?' I growled.

Glancing down at the speedometer, I saw that we were now doing 75mph.

The Land Rover thundered down the side of us.

Jack started to bark, sensing the growing anxiety in the truck.

'It's all right, boy,' I reassured him. 'Just some nutter trying to put the frighteners on us, that's all.'

With that, the Land Rover smashed into the side of the truck knocking us sideways.

'Jesus!' I yelled angrily.

Annie gasped. 'Frank!'

'It's all right,' I said as I gripped the steering wheel and got control back.

'What the hell are they playing at?'

'No bloody idea,' I said as I glanced over at her. 'Hold on really tight.'

Checking all the mirrors, I went to slam on the brakes hard.

From out of a field on our left, a tractor appeared as if from nowhere.

I winced, gripping the steering wheel and stamping on the brakes.

I desperately tried to slow us down but also avoid crashing headlong into the huge tractor.

The truck skidded.

I tried to turn out of the skid, throwing the steering wheel left, then right.

It was no use. I'd lost control of the truck.

We were moving sideways and spinning.

'Jesus,' I gasped.

We hit the kerbside with a huge thud.

Suddenly the truck itself was turning over onto its right side.

The clang of metal.

My temple banged against the doorframe. I was dazed.

Then we were over and onto the roof and upside down.

I reached for Jack who whimpered.

For a moment, I tried to clear my head.

I could feel the warm trickle of blood on the side of my face.

Glancing over at Annie, I could see she wasn't moving.

'Annie?' I croaked.

I reached over and touched her arm.

Nothing.

'Annie!' I said, this time with more urgency.

But her eyes were closed and she still wasn't moving.

Chapter 28

It had been two hours since the crash. I was sitting in the waiting area in A&E while a doctor checked Annie over in a nearby examination room. Thankfully, she had regained consciousness a few minutes after the crash. The paramedics had arrived within ten minutes and whizzed her off to hospital. I'd checked Jack over and he seemed to be fine too.

With the help of a local farmer, I'd managed to pull the Ranger back over onto its tyres. After a quick inspection, it seemed that apart from dents and scratches, my truck was okay to drive. That was the beauty of a tough Ford Ranger.

I'd checked in with Caitlin quickly and was relieved that Rachel was well. The lovely dementia nurse, Liz, had visited and checked Rachel's blood pressure and pulse. She'd also taken a blood sample to keep a check on her medication.

Out of the corner of my eye, I spotted two figures approaching.

Annie was sitting in a wheelchair and a young female nurse was pushing her towards me.

'You didn't have to wait,' she said, shaking her head.

'Oh, is this your husband?' the nurse asked as she stopped the wheelchair beside me.

'More like a partner in crime,' Annie joked. 'This is my friend, Frank.'

'Annie's had a nasty bang to the head,' the nurse said. 'CT scan showed no signs of anything sinister but I do think she's got some concussion.'

Annie pushed down with her arms as she tried to stand.

'I really think you should stay in the wheelchair, Annie,' the nurse said gently.

'Sod that,' she grumbled. 'I'm not being wheeled to the car in this thing.'

I gave her a dubious look. 'I really think it would be safer for you to stay sitting down.'

'Nonsense,' she snorted as she continued to try and stand up. But then she clearly felt a bit dizzy and sat straight back down again. 'Ah yes. Maybe the wheelchair isn't such a bad idea after all.'

'Thank you,' I said to the nurse kindly. 'I'll take it from here.'

The nurse put her hand on Annie's shoulder. 'And remember, if you feel sick or very dizzy, you need to come back in to be checked over.'

'Yes. I will. Thank you.'

Taking hold of the handles, I pushed Annie down the corridor towards the main exit.

'This is embarrassing,' she muttered.

'Why?' I said, shaking my head. 'You've just been in a car accident.'

'Did you have someone look at the cut on your head?' she asked.

I arched my brows and smiled. 'Just a scratch.'

'Just a scratch, he says. Always the tough guy, eh?'

'Where there's no sense, there's no feeling, as my old mum used to say.'

Annie laughed. 'By the way, Ethan ran the plates of that Land Rover.'

'Any joy?' I asked.

We reached the large, glass automatic doors to the hospital which slid open as we went through.

'Bit of a strange one,' she said. 'The car was stolen from a police compound a few days ago. It had been confiscated from someone near Corwen. And that person is a convicted drug dealer.'

'Right,' I said with some frustration as we crossed the car park and got closer to my truck. 'I guess if we don't know who stole the Land Rover, we can't trace who ran us off the road.'

Chapter 29

Sam and I galloped across the fields at the back of our farmhouse. Pulling on Duke's reins, I slowed him down to wait for Sam to catch up. After the day I'd had, I wouldn't have wanted to be anywhere else but with my grandson out in this stunning landscape. The sun was starting to wane and move behind the jagged ridge of mountains. It had been a few months since the mountain tops of Eryri/Snowdonia had been dusted with snow. In the fading light of the day they seemed to be a deep plum colour, which I knew was just a trick of the refracted light.

Below the mountain tops were the caves where King Arthur is said to be still sleeping as he waits for his men to rescue Wales. My father had always told me that he hated anything to do with the Arthurian legends of North Wales. He claimed that King Arthur was 'bloody English' and wasn't to be celebrated. I wasn't sure where he got that from, but it was typical of my father to make a snap decision about someone or something and then remain completely obdurate about it for the rest of his life. I'd done my own research, especially after my father had passed. It seemed that the received wisdom was that King Arthur was very much Welsh through and through. It was only when the tales became bastardised by English writers such as Tennyson that there had ever been any doubt.

'Taid,' Sam called over as he brought Lleuad to a stop and then leaned forward to pat his white coat. 'Well, done boy.'

I checked my watch. I was due to call my supervisor over at the Eryri/Snowdonia National Park Authority headquarters in Betws-y-Coed. I worked part-time as a Park Ranger and tomorrow was a work day, so I needed to check in and see what was on the agenda.

'Better head back now, mate,' I said.

I'd left Caitlin in charge at home, with Annie chatting to Rachel as they watched the telly.

'Really?' Sam said, looking disappointed.

'Sorry, mate. We'll come out again tomorrow. Promise.'

'Okay.' Sam shrugged but I knew that he'd stay out here for hours. Maybe I should let him ride on his own. I knew that I was being over-protective of him, but he was my grandson. After what had happened to my son James, I guess I felt that having Sam at the house was some kind of second chance. I just hoped that I didn't spoil him. It was the direct opposite of the kind of parenting that my father had employed. That was the whole point, I supposed.

Pulling Duke's reins round, I dug my heels into his flank. 'Come on, boy,' I said loudly as we galloped back towards the farmhouse. Checking behind, I saw that Sam and Lleuad had tucked in behind us.

I sucked in a lungful of fresh air as we galloped, Duke's hooves throwing small clods of earth up into the air as we went.

Five minutes later, we arrived back and tethered our horses to the long wooden fence around the paddock.

I clapped Sam on the back as we turned and headed towards the farmhouse.

'It's about time we thought about getting you some food,' I said, 'although Annie has said that she prefers it when I don't cook. I'll ask your mum if she can do it.'

Sam couldn't help but smirk.

I gave him a mock look of offence. 'Don't you dare say a word, sunshine.'

As I said this, I could hear a strange buzzing sound in the air. At first, I thought it was something like a small private plane or a microlite. Looking up, I scanned the sky to see where the noise was coming from but couldn't see anything.

'There it is, Taid,' Sam said, pointing to something that was barely visible. And it was low down in the sky, probably only a hundred to a hundred and fifty feet up.

'Oh yeah, I see it, mate,' I said with a nod as I put the flat of my hand above my eyes to shield them from the daylight.

'That's a drone, isn't it?' he asked.

'Looks like one,' I replied, 'although I'm no expert.'

'That bloody thing has been buzzing over this house for the past hour,' said an angry voice from behind us.

It was Caitlin.

'Over this house?' I asked to clarify.

'Yes.' Caitlin folded her arms and looked annoyed. Jack trotted by her side protectively before coming over to Sam who made a fuss of him.

'What's it doing, Taid?' Sam asked as he crouched down to stroke Jack's head.

'I'm not sure, mate,' I said calmly, but I could see that the drone had spooked Caitlin. 'I'm guessing it's something to do with mapping boundaries. Or some kind of geological survey.' I had no idea, and was making stuff up so as not to worry him.

Caitlin gestured to the farmhouse. 'Sam, why don't you go and say hello to Nain and Annie and then grab yourself a snack.'

I wagged my finger at Sam playfully. 'And do <u>not</u> eat all the Penguins,' I joked.

Sam pulled a face. 'Ew. I don't even like Penguins. They're gross.'

'Gross!' I snorted and shook my head. 'What is the world coming to?' I frowned. 'Then who keeps eating them all?'

Caitlin raised her hand. 'Guilty as charged, I'm afraid.'

'Mum! What are you like?' Sam laughed as he turned and made his way up the path towards the farmhouse.

Jack sat at my feet and looked up expectantly as if waiting to hear what Caitlin and I were about to talk about.

'You look worried,' I said, spotting Caitlin's concerned face as she scoured the air for the drone.

It honed into view again, and this time passed over our heads and then over the roof of the farmhouse before arcing back again in a wide loop.

'I've been watching it,' she said. 'It hasn't been anywhere else but here. Just around and around the house and the annexe.'

I took a few seconds to process this. It definitely did sound strange, even suspicious.

'Someone's watching the house, Dad. I know they are,' she said under her breath.

'Maybe,' I said as I watched the drone go out across the fields before stopping. 'You think TJ might be behind this?'

If TJ was planning anything up here, using a drone

might be a way of seeing what was going on at the farmhouse.

'Fuck this,' Caitlin snapped angrily and she turned and stormed away.

I watched her go before shielding my eyes to check on the drone again. I wasn't an expert, but whoever was in control of it had to be relatively close. The basic drones that we used to check Eryri/Snowdonia National Park for such things as broken fences or damaged dry stone walls only had a range of less than half a mile.

'Right, here we go,' Caitlin snarled as she stormed out of the farmhouse. She was holding the shotgun I'd given her and she was checking that there were cartridges inside.

'Erm, I'm not sure that's a good idea,' I said cautiously.

'Why not? The drone is on private property and scaring me, my mother, and my son,' she snapped.

'I don't think that's trespassing, but I admire your balls for grabbing the shotgun.'

She gave me a withering look. 'You can't say that kind of stuff these days, Dad.'

'Can't I? Oh, sorry. It's hard to keep up at my age.' I pointed up to the sky. 'Anyway, as they say in all my favourite westerns, shoot now and ask questions later …'

Just as I finished my sentence, Caitlin fired two shots over my head at the drone in quick succession.

CRACK! CRACK!

I JUMPED out of my skin as I wasn't prepared. 'Jesus, Caitlin!'

'Take that, you fucker!' she yelled.

I scanned the sky to see the drone still hovering.

'Bollocks,' she muttered.

But then the drone tipped a little, spun, and then just

fell out of the sky and dropped like a stone into the field next to us.

'Good shot,' I laughed, but then I saw something or someone moving over in the woods to our right.

I peered intently.

It looked as if someone was moving through the trees in a hurry. My instinct, given the timing, was that they were connected to the drone.

'Right, wait there,' I said to Caitlin as I jogged away down the path towards the paddock.

'Where are you going, Dad?' she called after me.

I turned back and pointed to her shotgun. 'Actually, give me that. Got any more shells?'

She nodded, then reached into her pocket and gave me a handful of red shotgun cartridges. 'What are you doing, Dad?'

I didn't answer.

Opening the heavy wooden gate, I charged across the paddock to Duke. Once I'd untethered him, I slotted the shotgun into the long leather holster, put my foot into the stirrup and pushed up into the saddle.

Pulling on the reins, I dug my heels into his sides hard.

'Come on, boy!' I shouted urgently.

Duke responded immediately and we galloped out of the paddock at speed and into the fields beyond.

If TJ really was involved in sending a drone over our farmhouse, I needed to find him or whoever was responsible.

Duke hit full gallop, and I took it in turns to swap hands on the reins as I pulled on my leather riding gloves.

I fixed my eyes roughly on where I'd seen movement amongst the trees.

At this speed it would take less than two minutes to gallop across the field to that point.

The woods had enough paths and spaces between the trees for me and Duke to have plenty of room.

I gripped the reins as Duke thundered on.

The rhythmic noise of his hooves was loud.

My pulse was now racing.

My eyes scanned the woods again, searching for any sign of movement.

Nothing.

Maybe I was too late.

But then out of the corner of my eye, I saw fluttering in the undergrowth. A few lower branches and their leaves shook.

Got you, you bastard! I thought.

Whoever it was in the woods clearly saw or heard me approaching as they started to move quicker.

I urged Duke on. 'Come on, boy!'

A few seconds later, we entered the woods and daylight vanished under the canopy of trees.

We slowed to a trot. It was too dangerous to go any faster.

My eyes strained through the trees, looking to where I'd seen movement.

Nothing.

I slowed Duke to a stop.

It was silent apart from Duke's laboured breathing.

A bird came out of a nearby tree and swooped past us, its wings clattering loudly. With its silvery and black colouring it looked like a hooded crow.

Then silence.

I nudged Duke forward again, his hooves crunching softly on the leaves and twigs on the pathway.

Where the hell are you?

My heart was pounding against my chest.

Over to our right a branch moved.

I pulled the reins and we stopped again.

Then I saw him.

A man in his 30s with blond hair under a black baseball cap.

He wasn't more than 30 yards away.

Kicking Duke, we sped to a canter as I ducked to avoid some low hanging branches.

The man clearly decided that hiding and creeping around was useless.

Coming out of the undergrowth, he sprinted away down the wide pathway.

'Come on,' I encouraged Duke with a sharp dig of my heels.

Within seconds we were hurtling after him, hooves thundering on the ground below us.

The man glanced back anxiously. I got a clear sight of his face.

We were now only twenty yards away.

He was running like his life depended on it.

Fifteen yards.

My plan was to use Duke to knock him to the ground and then jump down and confront him.

If what he'd been doing was perfectly innocent, there was no way he'd be running.

Suddenly, he darted left. He sprinted between two narrows trees and leapt across a ditch.

Bollocks!

I pulled Duke to a stop.

I'd have to go on foot.

I dismounted and set off after him, charging through the narrow trees and trying to leap the ditch.

Catching my foot against an exposed root, I tumbled to the ground.

I took the weight of the fall on my shoulder and back.

Bollocks!

I struggled to get to my feet, and tried to get my breath. In the old days I'd have leapt over that ditch without hesitation.

I heard an engine start from somewhere.

I jogged forwards, but my knee felt sore from the fall and slowed me down.

There was a clearing up ahead.

A white transit van started to pull away.

I stopped, trying to get my breath. I had no chance of catching him now.

I squinted at the number plate and tried to remember it. Maybe it was the same van that had been up to the farmhouse, pretending to be a lost delivery driver.

Oscar, Bravo, One, Three, Yankee, Zebra, Alpha.

Blowing out my cheeks, I made my way back to where Duke was standing. I pulled myself back up into the saddle and made my way home.

Chapter 30

Annie poured herself another large glass of Merlot, making a mental note to herself not to drink anymore, especially if she had concussion. She'd noticed in the past two days that combined with the codeine in her painkillers, the alcohol had not only taken away most of the pain in her knee, but also made her sleep better. But she was aware that this was a slippery slope. She'd known friends who'd become hooked on opiate painkillers and they'd had a terrible time trying to reduce the dose and come off them.

Sitting herself back down on her sofa, Annie grabbed the laptop that she'd been using for the past hour. On the television, the BBC's *Newsnight* was burbling away in the background but she wasn't really paying attention. Twenty years earlier, she would have been glued to all the news programmes on the television. Working as a High Court Judge not only meant keeping abreast of all the judicial changes, but also legislation. She prided herself on being very politically aware. But now she didn't seem to care that much. What had happened to her sister Meg, her nephew Callum, and her husband

Stephen, had turned her world upside down. She wasn't sure that she'd ever get over it. And the ego, arrogance, and pettiness of modern politicians seemed even more galling as a result.

Annie had been spending her time digging around in both Andrew Burrows and Sarah Meadows' lives. She and Frank had taken on board what the GP Judy Thompson had told them about Tina Lott. Her apparent 'resurrection' from the dead, the anger of her family - especially Beccy - and Andrew and Sarah's involvement as doctor and paramedic. Annie wanted to double check. What if this wasn't the only connection? What if there was something else?

Having taken some tips and hacks from Ethan, Annie was searching the General Register Office online – the GRO – which was a database of all UK births.

A quick search revealed that Andrew Edward Burrows was born at Glan Clwyd Hospital on September 28th 1989, making him thirty-three when he died. Sarah Louise Meadows was born on the 9th November 1989, also in Glan Clwyd Hospital, and also making her thirty-three when she died. Same age, born in the same hospital? Was that a coincidence? Thirty years as a Crown Court Judge had taught her that coincidences were very rare. Even Frank had told her that according to any detective worth his salt, coincidences just don't exist.

Armed with this information, she decided to dig further. Where did they live as children, and where did they go to school? A quick text to Ethan revealed that there was a website called Search My Past which could access school records.

After a few false starts, Annie used Andrew's full name and date of birth and found that he attended Ysgol y Mynydd, Dolgellau - translated as the Mountain School -

between 2000 and 2018. Then she typed in Sarah Louise Meadows, plus her date of birth.

Sarah Meadows' school appeared.

Ysgol y Mynydd – 2000-2018.

Taking a sip of her wine, Annie frowned. Andrew and Sarah were in the same year in the same school. They must have known each other.

She had no idea what the relevance was, but she picked up her phone. She needed to tell Frank.

Chapter 31

Taking a blanket from the end of the sofa, I walked over to Rachel, who had fallen asleep reading her book in the armchair, and placed it carefully over her. Caitlin was scrolling through her phone while Sam watched football on the television. Jack was curled up next to Sam, as if sensing that he was the smallest and youngest, and therefore most in need of protection.

I watched Rachel intently for a few seconds. The lovely wrinkles on her face. The smattering of freckles on the bridge of her nose. What I would give to have the 'old Rachel' back. Anything. Everything. I just wanted her to wake up in the morning and be back to her normal self. Making jokes, laughing, so full of life.

I reached out to move a stray strand of hair from her face. Then I took her reading glasses off.

'What are you thinking, Dad?' Caitlin asked gently.

I shook my head. 'I was just thinking about what your mother used to be like.'

'I do that too, but I try not to dwell on it.'

'Hard not to.'

'Do you want another whiskey?' she asked.

I shook my head. My mind was now latched onto another thought.

'You can get Facebook on your phone, can't you?' I asked as I moved across the room.

She gave me a slightly patronising smile. 'Yes, Dad. I can get Facebook on my phone.'

I went over and sat down next to her.

'Why, what are you thinking?' she asked.

'Is TJ on Facebook?'

'Yes, of course. Everyone is.'

'I'm not.'

She laughed. 'No, you're not.'

'The man I saw in the woods. The man who was driving a white transit van that looked just like the one that the lost delivery driver was driving yesterday ...'

'Yes. What are you getting at?'

'If he's a friend of TJ,' I said, thinking out loud, 'won't he be on TJ's Facebook thingy?'

'Bit of a longshot but definitely worth a try.'

She started to tap away at her phone, showing me the screen as she went. She shook her head angrily as she got to TJ's homepage. 'It still says that he's in a relationship with me. Deluded wanker.'

I sighed. 'Sorry, maybe this wasn't the best idea.' I didn't want Caitlin getting upset by looking at TJ's social media. But we did need to know if he was observing the farmhouse, or using one of his mates to do it.

'Don't be silly,' Caitlin reassured me. 'This is important ... He hasn't posted on here for months.' She then clicked onto TJ's friends and over 500 names came up. We scrolled through them slowly, looking carefully at each photo in case it was the blond-haired man that we'd both seen. After about five minutes, we got to the end of TJ's Facebook friends and there was no sign of him.

'Oh well,' I groaned. 'It was worth a look.'

'To be fair,' Caitlin said, 'people don't really post that much on Facebook these days.'

'Don't they?'

'Well, middle-aged and older people do,' she explained, 'but it's seen as a bit old fashioned.'

'Well, where is the hip place to post your social media then?' I asked.

She looked at me with a smirk. 'Hip? Bloody hell, Dad.'

I smiled and gave a shrug. 'I don't know. 'Cool' then.'

'It's all about 'the gram' these days.'

I raised a quizzical eyebrow. "The gram' being?'

'Instagram?'

'Oh yes. Even I've heard of Instagram,' I conceded.

'Here we go,' she said, turning the phone screen for me to look at as she scrolled down TJ's posts.

Then I saw a photo of a group of lads in a bar, and recognised a face at the back.

'There,' I said as I pointed to it.

She stopped, peered at the screen, and then nodded. 'Nice spot, Dad. That's the bastard.'

'Can you tell who he is or what his name is?' I asked.

'If TJ has tagged him in I can.'

'And I'll pretend I know what that means,' I joked.

'Got it,' she said triumphantly. 'Dean Ashgrove. I've never heard of him.'

I gave her a serious look. 'I'm afraid we're going to have to think of moving you and Sam out temporarily until I can fix this.'

Her face fell. 'Really?'

'Think about it,' I said gently. 'TJ's mate has been up here pretending to be a delivery driver. And today he was flying a bloody drone over the house. TJ is planning something.'

'I know he came up here drunk with a knife, but I don't think he'd actually do anything really stupid,' she said.

I reached out and put my hand on hers. 'But he used to hit you, didn't he? And in my experience, that type of thing only gets worse over the years, not better. I'm not taking any risks. And what about Sam?'

'How do you mean?'

I looked directly at her. 'Tell me honestly, can you categorically say that TJ and this Dean wouldn't come up here and take Sam?'

The blood visibly drained from her face. Then her eyes filled with tears. 'I'm so sorry about all this, Dad. It's all my fault.'

I put my arm around her. I hated to see her upset. 'It's not your fault. TJ is a prick, but that's not your responsibility, is it?'

'But I chose him to be with and to have a child with,' Caitlin said with a sniff as she wiped the tears from her face.

'We all make mistakes, love,' I reassured her gently.

'But where would we go? I don't want Sam to have to change schools.'

'He won't,' I said. 'I know someone who has just bought a lovely 4-bedroomed house not far from here.'

'Annie?'

'Yes, and I know she'd be more than happy to have you and Sam there for a bit.'

Chapter 32

It was 7am as I opened the door and saw that Rachel was propped up in bed. She was wearing her glasses and reading her book.

'I brought you a cuppa,' I said as I headed over to put the steaming mug of tea on her bedside table.

'You are a dear.'

'I am a dear, aren't I?' I chortled.

She gave me a quizzical smile. 'Biscuits?'

I frowned. 'Bit early for biscuits.'

She pulled an amused face. 'Nonsense. How could it ever be too early for biscuits?'

'Fair point,' I said with a smile. 'What are you reading?'

'Another one of those crime books,' she said, holding up the cover. 'They're set on Anglesey so it's really nice to read about somewhere we've been. And, of course, there's nothing like a good murder.'

I chortled. 'I'm not sure about that, but each to their own.' I looked at her intently. Her eyes were clear, bright, and sharp with intelligence. It felt like I'd got her back for these few seconds and I felt overwhelmed.

'What were those books we both liked to read, Frank?' she asked.

'Linda La Plante.'

She nodded. 'That's it. Prime Suspect. DI Tennyson. Christ, she had bigger balls than most of the detectives that she worked with.'

I burst out laughing. 'She did. I guess she had to, working in The Met in the 80s.'

'The Met. Institutionally misogynistic and racist in those days,' she said.

'True. Wasn't any better up here though, was it?' I realised that this was the most lucid conversation that I'd had with my wife in weeks – maybe months.

'No. Definitely not,' she said with an ironic laugh.

There was noise from outside on the landing.

I'd arranged to drop Caitlin and Sam's things over at Annie's before taking Sam on to school.

Rachel gestured to the door. 'What's going on out there?'

'Long story, but Caitlin and Sam are going to say at Annie's for a bit. But there's no need to worry, love,' I reassured her.

She looked confused. 'Sam? Who's Sam?'

'Our grandson, Sam,' I said slowly, fearing that the lucid, articulate, Rachel had just slipped away in the blink of an eye.

She looked perplexed. 'But we don't have a grandson. How can we?'

I glanced at her face and she was gone. The vile, loathsome, disease that was slowly destroying her brain was back. It wasn't fair.

Feeling a mixture of sadness and anger, I took a long breath to steady myself.

'It's fine,' I reassured her. 'I'll pop and get those biscuits for you, shall I?'

She nodded, completely oblivious to the conversation that we'd just had. 'That would be lovely. I don't know what I'd do without you, Frank.'

I walked over to the door and then glanced back to see her reading her book.

Chapter 33

Having dropped Caitlin and Sam's overnight stuff at Annie's house, I was now taking Sam over to his primary school in Dolgellau. The plan was for Caitlin to stay with her mother while I wasn't at the farmhouse. Annie or I would collect Sam from school and take him to Annie's. It seemed to be that the most likely time for anything to happen was during the night as that would be when we were most vulnerable. I was always at home in the evenings and during the night, which meant that Sam and Caitlin could be at Annie's out of harm's way. Either way, the whole thing needed to be resolved in the next few days if it could be. I was determined that neither Caitlin or Sam were going to have their lives disrupted by a scumbag like TJ. He'd done enough damage when they were living with him in London.

Sam sat next to me in the cab of the Ford Ranger with Jack between us. He had his hand almost permanently on Jack's head, stroking it.

'You okay, mate?' I asked him as we entered Dolgellau.

'Fine.'

'I'm sorry about the upheaval, but it shouldn't be for more than a few days.'

'That's okay. I like Annie. It's like I've got two Nains,' he said innocently. 'Is this something to do with my dad?'

'Sort of, but it's nothing to worry about.'

'I know.' He shrugged and then pointed to the stereo. 'Can I put some music on?'

'Help yourself.'

'I'm not playing your music, Taid,' he announced as he shuffled through the radio stations.

'I thought you loved country music, Sam?' I said, teasing him.

'No,' he said indignantly. He found a song that he liked – *As It Was* by *Harry Styles* – and turned the volume up.

The song was melodic and catchy.

'Who's this then?' I asked.

'Harry Styles.'

'Oh, I think I've heard of him.'

He gave me a dubious look as he sang along.

About two minutes later, we pulled into the school car park and I stopped the truck.

Sam took off his seatbelt.

'I'm going to jump out with you, mate. I need to explain to your teacher that it'll be either me, Annie, or your mum who picks you up from school.'

'Okay.'

'What's her name again?'

'Miss Gates,' he said as we wandered through the car park.

I couldn't help but give the surrounding area a quick scan to check there was no one suspicious lurking around. It was hard to tell, as there were parents and children everywhere.

Sam pointed to a young woman in her 20s who was

standing holding a mug of tea just outside the main doors. 'There she is.'

'What's she like?' I asked under my breath as we approached.

'Strict,' he answered, pulling a face.

I smiled at him. 'Good.'

'Bore da, Sam,' Miss Gates said in a bright singsong voice as we arrived. It was Welsh for good morning.

'Bore da, Miss.'

She gestured to the doors. 'Go on in, Sam.'

I gave Miss Gates a meaningful look. 'I wondered if I could have a quick word?'

'Of course,' she said in a suitably serious tone.

'My daughter and Sam's dad aren't together. And I'm afraid Sam's dad, known as TJ, is on bail at the moment. I have reason to believe that he could be living around here and might try to make contact with Sam or even pick him up.'

Miss Gates nodded. 'Okay. I'm not sure that the school was aware of all this.'

'It's a very recent development. The only people who can pick up Sam are me, his mother, and his Auntie Annie. No one else.'

'Okay, I'll make a note of this. Obviously, we take safeguarding very seriously,' she said quietly as other parents and children arrived. 'If Sam's mum can put all that in an email to the Head as well that would be very useful.'

'I'm sure she can do that. And thank you.'

Suddenly the air was filled with sharp, very loud, noises. To the untrained ear it sounded like fireworks.

CRACK! CRACK! CRACK!

Miss Gates looked at me in shock and asked, 'Oh my God. What's that?'

I was already heading for the doors.

'I used to be a police officer,' I said. 'Those were gunshots. You need to ring 999 and put the school into lockdown immediately!'

With my heart pounding, I ran through the doors into the school.

Another gunshot. CRACK!

There were some screams as children fled up a corridor and into various classrooms.

I needed to find Sam.

'Taid!' a voice shouted from behind me.

I spun round and saw Sam and some other pupils standing looking terrified by the door to a classroom.

'Right, mate. I need you and your friends to come in here,' I said, trying to remain calm as I ushered them inside. 'Close the door behind you, and barricade it with tables and chairs. Sit on the floor and don't stand up or go to the door until I come back. Okay?'

Sam looked anxious but nodded.

'Good lad.' I touched his arm reassuringly then turned and ran from the classroom, hearing the door slam behind me.

CRACK!

There was more screaming. Kids running into classrooms.

'Everyone get into the classrooms!' I shouted to the various pupils who were peering nervously down the corridor.

'What's going on?' asked a young male teacher.

'Those are gunshots,' I told him. 'Get your class into that room, barricade the door and stay on the floor. Ring 999 and tell them you need armed officers.'

He nodded nervously as he followed my orders and disappeared inside the classroom.

I continued to direct everyone into the nearest vacant rooms.

A female teacher looked out nervously.

'Close and barricade the door! Sit on the floor and don't move!' I barked.

She nodded and slammed the door.

CRACK!

Within a few seconds, the corridor was clear of teachers and pupils.

I jogged down it, checking that all the doors were closed as I went. Then I grabbed my phone and rang the number for Dolgellau CID.

'CID,' said a voice.

'This is retired Detective Inspector Frank Marshal …'

'How can I help?' asked the voice.

'There is an active shooting at St Mark's Primary School in Dolgellau,' I said quietly as I noticed that the main cafeteria was to my right. 'I've no idea if there are any casualties but I've advised them to put the school in lockdown. We need armed officers asap. I've got to go …'

I ended the call and then listened carefully as I crept slowly into the cafeteria.

Then I stopped.

There was a low groaning noise coming from somewhere.

Moving swiftly from table to table, I suddenly saw a woman's shoes and feet.

Someone was lying on the floor on the far side.

Dashing over, I saw a woman in her 30s whom I assumed was a teacher.

She had been shot three or four times in the torso and was soaked in dark red blood.

Jesus Christ!

I took off my coat quickly and rolled it up, then I knelt

beside her and used it to see if I could stem the bleeding. I knew it wasn't likely.

She whimpered as she looked at me. She was shaking and terrified, and there was blood coming from her mouth and nostrils.

'It's okay,' I reassured her as I grabbed my phone with one hand and tapped 999. 'We're going to get you an ambulance, okay?'

I put my hand on her shoulder to try and reassure her, but she was struggling to breathe. She coughed, and more blood came from her mouth. One of the bullets had hit a lung.

'Emergency, which service do you require?' said the operator.

'Ambulance,' I said quietly.

The injured woman made direct eye contact with me. Her face was contorted with pain and fear.

I held her hand and squeezed it.

'Ambulance service, what is your emergency?'

'I have a female teacher with multiple gunshot wounds,' I said. 'We're at St Mark's Primary School in Dolgellau, North Wales. I'm a retired police officer. The school is in lockdown.'

'Is the patient breathing?'

'Yes, but she's lost a lot of blood.'

'Do you know how old she is?'

'Mid 30s I think.' I could see that she was clinging on to life and struggling to breathe. I felt her hand contracting with the terrible strain.

'Is she conscious?'

Her eyes were wild with panic, and then her hand went completely limp.

Oh God, no.

'Hello caller. Is the patient conscious?'

I reached over to feel her neck for a pulse.

Nothing.

Who the hell has done this! I thought angrily.

'Hello caller?'

'I'm sorry but I think she's gone. She doesn't have a pulse,' I said in a virtual whisper.

'I'm sorry to hear that. If you can stay on the line, there is an ambulance on the way …'

Suddenly, I heard a clatter from the kitchen area on my left.

Someone's in there.

Maybe it was someone hiding.

Getting up slowly, I moved towards the counter and serving area that divided the cafeteria and the kitchen area behind.

I could see a figure hiding behind one of the industrial washers. Maybe it was a pupil or a teacher.

'Hello,' I whispered.

The figure jumped out to face me.

They were wearing a hoodie and balaclava.

Shit!

They raised a handgun and fired a shot straight at me.

I ducked and the bullet whistled past my ear.

Then they turned and sprinted away towards the fire exit doors to the rear of the kitchen.

I had no choice but to pursue them. They were now responsible for three cold, brutal murders in the community that I'd grown up in.

I climbed over the counter, ran across the kitchen and out of the fire exit doors which led to the side of the school's car park and then playing field.

As I glanced right, I saw that the figure was now sprinting through the car park.

I set off in pursuit. There was the sound of approaching sirens.

The figure glanced back at me.

Pumping my arms, I weaved in and out of the cars, sucking in breath as I went.

Up ahead, there was a high mesh fence.

The figure stopped at the fence and then turned back to face me again.

Oh shit. Here we go.

Raising the gun, they fired another shot and I instinctively dived to the ground.

I landed on my hip bone which was incredibly painful.

'Argh, bloody hell!'

I rolled over and looked up.

The figure had already scaled the mesh fence and was now easing themselves down the other side.

I scrambled to my feet and ran towards the fence.

The figure dropped down the other side but landed heavily and seemed to go over on their ankle.

They let out a groan.

Glancing back at me, we made eye contact before they turned and limped away.

I looked up at the mesh fence. There was no way I could get over that and catch them up now.

Bollocks, I thought in frustration.

Then my mind went back to the poor teacher who had died in front of me. Who the hell was carrying out all these shootings, and why? They needed to be stopped before they destroyed another life.

Chapter 34

An hour later and the whole area around the school was awash with emergency service vehicles. Blue lights were flashing, and the crackle of police radios filled the air. A team of armed response officers – dressed in their black Kevlar bulletproof vests, helmets, carrying Heckler & Koch semi-automatic machine guns – had been deployed. Now the hunt for the killer was on, whoever they were.

The air was suddenly filled with the thundering sound of rotor blades. I glanced up into the sky and saw a black and yellow Airbus H145 helicopter that had been deployed by the National Police Air Service – NPAS. It was hovering and circling over an area about 50 yards away where I'd told officers I'd seen the killer escaping. About twenty minutes ago, I'd seen the Police Canine Unit being deployed in the same area.

I took a breath as I stood lost in thought close to where I'd dropped off Sam and spoken to Miss Gates. It was hard to believe what had happened in this primary school in the quiet town of Dolgellau since then. The paramedics had confirmed what I already knew - that the poor teacher had died from the gunshot wounds. The whole of the school had been sealed off, and now police officers and teachers were escorting the pupils out slowly so they could be taken away by waiting parents. Some of the children were in tears when they came out. Others just looked stunned and in deep shock by what had happened.

Then I saw Sam coming towards me. Even though I knew he was safe, it was still a relief to see him.

'Taid,' he said quietly as he came over.

I gave him a hug and then crouched down and looked at him. He blinked as if he couldn't quite take in what had happened.

'Are you okay, mate?' I asked him, putting my hand on his shoulder.

He nodded but I wasn't convinced.

I pointed to my truck which was parked twenty yards away. 'Come on. I'll take you over to Annie's.'

'Where's Mum?' he asked.

'It's okay. I called her to say that you're safe. She's going to meet you at Annie's.'

Then he looked up at me in bewilderment. 'Is Mrs Richards really dead?'

I took a moment before I answered. 'Yes she is, Sam. I'm really sorry.'

I opened the passenger door and watched him get in and give Jack a big hug. Over to my right, I saw an unmarked car pull up. I recognised it as the one that Dewi and Kelly used.

'I'll be back in a minute, mate,' I said to Sam as I slammed the door shut.

Kelly got out of the car and looked over at me with a grim expression.

I gave her a nod and decided to go over.

She gestured to the school. 'I hear you were right in the middle of this?'

'That's right. I'd just dropped Sam off when I heard gunshots. Then I found Mrs Richards ...' I shook my head. 'She died right in front of me.'

Kelly gave me an empathetic look. 'God, Frank. That's tough.'

'Unless you stop them, they're going to continue killing, you do know that?' I said with a sense of urgency.

'I'm all too aware of that, Frank.' Kelly narrowed her eyes. 'Do you know anything that we don't know?'

I hesitated for a moment.

Kelly sighed. 'Come on, Frank. I know you don't trust Dewi but he's not around. I just think we need to work together on this before someone else gets killed.'

I nodded in agreement. Kelly was a good copper and what she'd said made sense.

'We thought that Andrew Burrows and Sarah Meadows were targeted due to an incident involving a woman called Tina Lott,' I explained.

Kelly gave a shrug to indicate the name didn't ring a bell.

'She was pronounced dead by Sarah at her home, and then by Andrew,' I continued. 'She was suffering from a rare disorder called Lazarus Syndrome. Tina was taken to the mortuary at Glan Clywd but her heart restarted. Professor Fillery discovered that she was still alive when he went to start the post-mortem.'

'Oh God, that's horrible. What happened?'

'They rushed her to the ICU but she died. Her daughter, Beccy, was incredibly angry and has pursued a legal claim for negligence.'

Kelly thought for a second. 'Well, there's certainly motive there.'

I gestured over to the school. 'I've no idea how Mrs Richards fits into all this though,' I said, feeling confused. 'There's something else too,' I added.

'Go on.'

'Andrew and Sarah were both born in the same year, 1989, at Glan Clwyd Hospital, and were in the same year at Ysgol y Mynydd …'

'Yeah, I did know that actually.'

'Right,' I said.

'I went to that school but I was two years younger,' Kelly said and then frowned. 'I just assumed that everyone in Dolgellau was born in Glan Clwyd Hospital and went to the local secondary school. I thought it was a coincidence that they were the same age that's all.'

I gave Kelly a look. 'It might be,' I said dubiously.

She narrowed her eyes at me. 'Don't tell me. I'm a police officer so I shouldn't believe in coincidences?'

'Something like that,' I said dryly. Then I looked back at the school. 'What about Mrs Richards?'

Kelly shrugged and then shook her head. 'I don't know much about her yet.'

'I think she taught Year 6,' I said as I spotted Miss Gates standing by a uniformed officer. It looked like she'd been giving a statement. 'Let's find out.'

I moved slowly over to where she was standing. She was visibly upset.

'Miss Gates,' I said softly.

The officer, in his 40s, looked at me. 'Frank Marshal, isn't it?'

'That's right.'

'I heard you chased after the shooter,' he said, shaking his head. 'I can't work out if that was bloody reckless or just very brave.'

'Neither can I,' I admitted with a self-effacing expression. 'Okay if I have a quick word with Miss Gates?'

'No problem, Frank. We've just finished up here.'

He moved away, clearly explaining to a couple of other younger officers who I was. I hoped that what he was saying was complimentary. At the risk of being egotistical, I was pretty certain that it was.

'Hi Miss Gates,' I said, looking at her pale face that was red and puffy from where she'd been crying.

Kelly took out her notebook and pen as she came to stand next to me.

'I'm so sorry about what's happened this morning,' Kelly said gently.

Miss Gates nodded and I could tell from her eyes that she was still in shock.

She sniffed and then took a deep breath. 'I don't understand how this could have happened.'

'I know this has been horrendous for you,' I said quietly, 'but there's just a couple of things I'd like to ask you about Mrs Richards that might really help us.'

'Of course,' she whispered, still looking bewildered.

'Could you tell us what her first name was?' I asked.

'Louise,' she replied, trying to hold it together but still shaking.

'And was Richards her married name?' Kelly asked.

'Yes. Her maiden name was Dyer.'

'Louise Dyer,' I said. Then I turned to look at Kelly.

Her expression had changed. She nodded.

'Louise Dyer was in the same year at school as Andrew Burrows and Sarah Meadows,' she said, pointing out the significance.

Chapter 35

I'd picked Annie up at 12pm. Caitlin had driven herself and Sam back over to the farmhouse to be with Rachel. I'd given Caitlin strict instructions to keep her shotgun close to hand and not to hesitate to use it. I'd also left Jack there, so God help anyone who started to snoop around or pose any kind of threat.

Annie and I were now heading to Brithdir, a small hamlet on the outskirts of Dolgellau and close to Llanfachreth. I knew Brithdir because it had a famous church, St Mark's, although I was pretty sure that it was no longer open. The church was still considered to be one of the finest Arts and Crafts churches in Wales. I remembered learning about it at school, and given that was back in the early 60s, it was a miracle.

Annie had remembered that she'd served as a parish councillor with Louise Richards' mother, Bev, about ten years ago. I felt that I owed it to Bev and Louise's family to let them know as sensitively as I could that I had been with Louise when she'd passed. It was important that they knew she hadn't been alone, that I was holding her hand, and that it was as peaceful as it could have been in the circumstances. It might also be a chance to ask some delicate questions.

We pulled up by the picturesque cottage, and I saw that there was already an unmarked navy Astra outside, along with a marked patrol car which I assumed the family liaison officer – FLO – had travelled in.

As I parked up on the grassy curb, Kelly and Ian came out of the front door. They were talking quietly to a woman in her 50s who Annie confirmed was Bev Dyer.

Annie grabbed hold of the flowers she had bought and we got out of the truck, making our way along the side of the small, rural road. We arrived at the garden gate, which squeaked as we opened it.

Kelly and Ian looked over at us as they bid Bev goodbye at the door.

'It would be nice to meet you both under nicer circumstances at some point,' Annie said quietly as we met them on the path.

Kelly took a breath. 'As you can imagine, she's devastated.'

'Of course,' I said sombrely. 'I wanted to let her know that I was with Louise this morning.'

Ian looked at me sympathetically. 'Yes, I assumed that's why you were here.'

Annie raised an eyebrow. 'Did Bev shed any light on anything that might be useful to us?'

'Not really.' Kelly pulled a face. 'I didn't want to probe too much but I'm aware that time is of the essence.'

Then something occurred to me as I looked at Ian. 'I've remembered where I know you from.'

'Go on,' he said with a slightly bemused look.

'You used to play cricket,' I said as I struggled to access my memory, 'as a teenager.'

He smiled. 'That's right.'

'Dolgellau Cricket Club,' I continued. 'You were one of the best batsmen I'd ever seen.'

He seemed a little self-conscious at my remark. 'I don't remember being that good, Frank.'

'We say batters these days, don't we?' Annie said, giving me a look.

'I don't … I used to do a bit of coaching. Under 10s,' I told Ian, realising that I hadn't thought about that for possibly decades.

'Yes, of course,' he said. 'I do remember now.'

'And your dad was involved down at the club, wasn't he?'

'That's right. He was the club secretary for a while.'

'Alan?'

'Yes. I'm afraid he died a couple of years ago,' he said sadly.

'Oh, I'm sorry to hear that. Did you ever keep it up? The cricket?'

'No, unfortunately. We moved away from the area for Dad's work. Maybe I'll pick it up again now I'm back.'

'Yes, you should definitely do that.'

I glanced at Annie who nodded towards the house.

'We'd better go and pay our condolences,' I said, gesturing to the front door that had been left slightly ajar.

'Let me know if you get anything,' Kelly said, 'before this maniac kills someone else.'

Annie and I turned and made our way up the garden path.

The front garden was neat and functional but could have done with a splash of colour somewhere.

Annie reached the door first and gave it a gentle knock.

A few seconds later, Bev appeared. Her face was without make-up and was puffy and red from where she'd been crying. She had on a crumpled cardigan and some black joggers.

Behind her, I saw the family liaison officer – female, 20s, – standing in the kitchen.

'Hello, Bev,' Annie said in no more than a whisper as she slowly handed her the flowers. 'I'm so sorry for your loss.'

Bev took a second to remember her and then said, 'Thank you, Annie.'

Annie then gestured to me. 'This is my friend, Frank Marshal.'

Bev's eyes widened a little. 'Frank Marshal?' Then she opened the door looking slightly overwhelmed. 'Please, please, come in.'

She clearly knew who I was, and that I'd been with her daughter that morning.

Chapter 36

Annie and I had been sitting opposite Bev in her living room for about five minutes when the door opened and a woman in her 30s came in with a tray of coffees which she put down on the coffee table. She had been introduced to us as Louise's older sister, Caz. I could see the family resemblance, except she had very bleached blonde hair and a tanned face.

'Here you go,' she said quietly, and then she turned to Bev. 'I've got to go now, Mum. To ... to the hospital.'

From the expressions on both their faces, it was obvious that Caz meant she was going to formally identify her sister's body.

Bev reached out and held Caz's hand. 'I can come with you, love.'

She shook her head. 'No, Mum. I can do this. You stay here in case people come round.'

Bev put her hand to her mouth as tears formed in the corners of her eyes.

'Anyway, it was nice to meet you,' Caz said to us. Then

she visibly took a long breath and walked slowly towards the door.

'You too,' I said. 'I wish it had been under better circumstances.'

As she left, there were a few seconds of silence.

I sipped at my black coffee and then looked over at Bev who wore a haunted expression.

'I thought I should come and see you,' I explained gently. 'I know the police told you that I was with Louise this morning.'

Bev nodded very slowly and her eyes filled with tears. 'Yes,' she whispered.

Annie reached into her jacket pocket, pulled out a small packet of tissues, and handed them to her. 'Here you go,' she said with an understanding smile.

'Thank you.' Bev sighed and wiped the tears from her eyes. 'I'm surprised that I've got any tears left. It's like some terrible nightmare that I wish I could just wake up from. I keep thinking that Lou is going to send me a text or ring me.'

Annie and I gave a nod of understanding. We'd both experienced horrible loss so we knew exactly how she felt.

I leaned forward. 'I thought I should tell you exactly what happened, but if you're not up to it …'

She sniffed and then blew out her cheeks. 'Please, I'd like to know.'

'When I arrived to drop my grandson off this morning, I heard the gunshots in the school. I went down the corridor and eventually came to the cafeteria,' I explained slowly. 'That's when I saw Louise. She had been shot and was lying on the ground.'

Bev closed her eyes for a second as if she couldn't bear to hear it.

'I went over to her and she looked up at me,' I continued in a virtual whisper, 'so I crouched down next to her.'

Bev looked directly at me as the tears rolled down her face. 'Was she scared?'

I gave a little shake of my head. The last thing I wanted to do was compound her grief by telling her that her daughter was terrified. 'No, she didn't seem to be scared. And then I sat with her and I held her hand as I rang for the ambulance.'

Bev gritted her teeth as her face twisted with grief. 'You … you held her hand?'

'Yes,' I said, 'and then I told her that she was okay, that I was with her, and that she wasn't alone. And …' I felt a lump in my throat, 'that was when she passed. And it was peaceful.'

Bev got up and came towards me. I stood up as she wrapped her arms around me and wept.

'Thank you. Thank you so much,' she sobbed. 'I'm so glad that she didn't die on her own, and that you were with her like that.'

'It was the least I could do,' I reassured her. She took a step back, blinked, and looked at me.

'It sounds silly, but that's going to be some comfort to me and my family,' she said.

We both sat down and there was a poignant silence for a few moments.

'If I can, I'd really like to help find the person who did this to your daughter,' I said quietly. 'I'm afraid that if we don't catch them soon, they are going to do this again.'

'Of course.' Bev gave a nod of understanding. 'I've told the police everything I know.'

Annie moved a strand of hair from her face. 'Would

you mind if Frank and I asked you a couple of questions? We're trying to help the police.'

Bev shook her head. 'No, that's fine, Annie.'

'Do you know if Louise knew Andrew Burrows or Sarah Meadows very well?'

'I don't think so. It had already crossed my mind.'

'But they did all go to school together?' I asked.

'Yes, but that was a long time ago.'

Annie raised an eyebrow. 'So, as far as you know, they didn't stay in touch after school?'

'No. If I remember correctly, they were all quite friendly when they were teens, but I guess they just found different friends as they grew older. And I think Andrew went off to university and moved away for some time.'

I scratched my beard as I processed all this. 'Can you think of anything else that might link them all? Mutual friend, a club, or a place that they all went?'

'No, I'm sorry. I'm pretty sure that Louise didn't have anything to do with Andrew or Sarah these days. She would have told me if she had. And she just never mentioned them.'

'Just out of interest, who was Louise's doctor?' I asked.

'Judy Thompson,' Bev replied.

Annie looked puzzled. 'Do the names Joseph, Tom, or Laura Reeves mean anything to you?'

'No, sorry.'

'What about Tina Lott or her daughter Beccy?' I enquired.

Bev shook her head. 'No.'

'Okay,' I said as Annie and I stood up. 'Thank you for seeing us. And again, I'm so sorry.'

'It was very kind of you to come here and tell me,' she reassured me as she showed us to the door.

'Goodbye Bev,' Annie said gently.

As we walked away down the garden path, I gave Annie a frustrated look.

What the hell was it that linked all three victims and had led to such violent deaths? It felt like we were back to square one again.

Chapter 37

'Hello again,' Judy Thompson said as she ushered Annie and I into her office.

Judy had offered to help us, and even though Louise Richards had been a teacher, we still wondered if there was any medical connection between her and the other two victims. It was the only strong lead we had to go on at the moment.

Annie and I sat down.

'We've just come from seeing Bev Dyer, Louise Richards' mother,' I began.

Judy shook her head in bewilderment. 'I can't believe any of this is happening. It's all over the news every time I turn on the radio or television. Louise's poor family.'

'Yes, they're obviously devastated.'

Judy narrowed her eyes and searched my face. 'I understand that you were caught up in the events this morning, Frank?'

'Yes. It was pretty horrific down at the school.'

'Someone told me that you'd actually chased the killer and that they'd shot at you?' she said, sounding surprised.

I shrugged. 'Slightly reckless on my part, but yes.'

Annie shot me a look. '<u>Slightly</u> reckless?'

'Annie, you thought that the person you'd seen shoot Andrew was a woman,' Judy said before glancing over at me. 'Did you have the same thought this morning, Frank?'

'Very difficult to tell.'

'Especially when you're trying to dodge bullets, I guess,' Annie said ironically.

'So you didn't get that opinion then?'

'I just couldn't tell,' I admitted.

Judy seemed to be pursuing this line of questioning more than seemed necessary. It felt odd.

'We understand that Louise Richards was your patient?' Annie said.

'That's right, she was.'

'Obviously we'd made the connection between Andrew, Sarah and what happened to Tina Lott,' I said, 'but unless you know any different, I can't see how Louise would be connected to that case?'

'No.' Judy shook her head. 'I can't think why she would either.'

Annie sat forward on her seat. 'The only thing that we can connect them with is that they were all in the same year at school.'

As I peered at Judy something occurred to me.

'Actually, I'm assuming that as you're local, you also went to Ysgol y Mynydd?' I didn't know why I hadn't thought of it before.

I could tell from the look on her face that she didn't like my question. 'Yes. I did,' she said, sounding very defensive as if I'd accused her of something.

That was weird.

'Oh right,' Annie said with slight surprise at her

changing tone. 'I hadn't thought of that. Did you know Andrew, Sarah and Louise from school then?'

Judy visibly took a breath. 'Yes,' she said a little sharply.

I sensed that something about our questions, or her memory of school, had unsettled her. 'You're about the same age as them, aren't you?' I asked.

She seemed to bristle. 'I'm exactly the same age as them. I was in the same year at school.'

I gave a quizzical frown. Not only did it seem weird that she had never mentioned this before, but her brusque manner was also curious and out of character.

'Oh right. So, you must have known them all?' Annie said with raised eyebrows.

'Not really.' Judy shook her head, sounding irritated. 'We weren't friends. And I don't think I shared any classes with them except when I was very young.' Then she glanced at her computer screen. 'I'm very sorry but my next appointment is waiting.'

That was our cue to leave.

Annie shot me a look as if to confirm that Judy's manner had been very strange when asked about knowing the victims at school. I just had no idea why.

Chapter 38

As Annie and I pulled out of the medical centre car park, I spotted a floral tribute over where Andrew Burrows had been shot and killed. I slowed the truck for a moment so we could take a respectful look.

'It's so strange,' Annie said very quietly. 'It feels so long ago since I watched the shooting but it's only been a matter of days.'

'Yes, it's all just happened so fast.' I turned to look at her. 'It's not just me, is it? Was Judy's behaviour really odd when we quizzed her about the fact that she'd known all three victims at school?'

'More than odd,' she said without hesitation as we started to pull out of the car park and towards the centre of Dolgellau. 'She seemed angry that we'd even asked her about it.'

We turned onto Lombard Street where the road was so narrow that there was only about a foot between the truck and the houses either side.

'It seemed as if she was hiding something,' I said, thinking out loud.

There were a few seconds of poignant silence.

'You don't think she has anything to do with the shootings, do you?' Annie asked.

'I can't see how.' I frowned. 'If I apply the basics of good detective work, which are motive, means and opportunity, then we fall down on motive straight away for starters.'

Turning out onto the Bala Road, I could see that there was black smoke rising up into the air in the distance. I assumed it was a bonfire or something innocuous.

'True. Yes, that doesn't make any sense does it, now I'm thinking about it,' Annie admitted, 'and I can't think why she would have any motive. But her behaviour was just so strange.'

'The whole school conversation definitely made her feel uncomfortable.'

Annie shrugged. 'Maybe Judy didn't have a very pleasant time at school and it was hard to talk about?'

'Maybe,' I said. 'I didn't enjoy my school days much to be honest. And I got bullied a bit.'

'No offence, but who the hell would dare bully you, Frank?'

'Actually, I was quite shy and sensitive as a boy,' I confessed. 'I looked up to some of the older more confident boys. I think they call it 'people pleasing' these days. I guess that made me a target. Just a bit of name calling and the odd punch in the face.'

The traffic was building up in front of us and slowing. The thick black smoke seemed to be coming from up ahead and over to our right.

Annie's eyes widened. 'The odd punch in the face. Oh, well that's all right then,' she said dryly with a shake of her head.

'It was the late 50s and early 60s. The world was a

different place.' Even now it made me feel a bit squirmy to think how sycophantic I'd been at times. 'Now that I look back,' I continued, deep in thought, 'I think my father's bullying and odd bouts of violence just knocked my confidence as a boy. And kids are very good at picking up on the vulnerabilities of others and then picking on them.'

As I said it out loud, I actually got a lump in my throat. I wasn't even sure that I'd ever articulated that thought before, let alone said it out loud.

Annie must have spotted me looking a little upset so she reached over and touched my forearm reassuringly.

I took a deep breath. 'God, sorry, I don't know where all that came from.' I felt slightly embarrassed.

'Don't apologise,' she said warmly. 'The one thing I've learned along the way is not to bottle stuff up. Get it off your chest, whatever it is.'

'Not something I'm very good at,' I admitted quietly.

The burst of a police siren broke my train of thought as the traffic moved and I saw what was causing the hold up and the smoke.

A car was on fire in the small car park over to our right.

There were several uniformed police officers directing traffic away from the area.

A fire engine, with its lights flashing, drove past us on the wrong side of the road before pulling right to park close to the fire.

'I wonder what's going on?' Annie said with a furrowed brow.

I shook my head and then spotted DC Ian Ramsey standing in the car park with his phone to his ear.

'I think I'm going to be nosey and stop and find out,' I said as I looked around for a side road to park in.

'You read my mind,' Annie said.

Indicating left, I pulled across the road, went down a small residential side street and parked up on the pavement.

Annie and I jumped out of the truck, walked up the road and crossed over.

There were two uniformed officers standing at the entrance to the car park. I didn't recognise either of them and they gave Annie and I a quizzical look.

One of them held up his hand, palm towards us. 'I'm sorry, I'm going to have to ask you both to cross back over the road please.'

'It's okay, constable,' said a voice, 'they're with me. You can let them through.'

It was Ian.

I gave him a nod as we walked over to where he was standing.

'Any idea what happened?' I asked him as Annie and I turned to look at the shell of the car. The flames were starting to dampen down.

Over to our right, firemen were unreeling hoses and starting to douse the car with water. The noise from the fire engine and the water spraying was loud.

'No. I just happened to be nearby when I saw the smoke,' he said, raising his voice. 'By the time I got over here, the car was up in flames but there was no one around.'

As the flames died down, I realised that the burning car was a Land Rover Defender.

I shot a look over at Annie.

'Isn't that the car that tried to run us off the road?' she said.

I moved around and saw that the first part of the licence plate was still intact – *YF1*.

'Same registration,' I said.

Ian frowned. 'Someone tried to run you off the road?'

I nodded and pointed to the burning car. 'I'm assuming it was the killer, and they were driving that car.'

Ian pointed around the area where we were located. 'Unfortunately, there aren't any CCTV cameras around here, but I'll get uniform to do a door-to-door to see if anyone saw anything.'

Chapter 39

As Annie and I drove up the bumpy driveway to my farmhouse, I saw Caitlin waving a shotgun at a woman who looked terrified. Jack was circling her and barking.

As I got closer, I realised that I recognised the woman.

'Oh God. What the hell is going on?' I exclaimed.

'Isn't that Caz Dyer?' Annie asked in astonishment.

'Yes,' I said apprehensively. I parked up and jumped out of the truck before something horrible happened. 'Woah! Caitlin, what are you doing?' I shouted as I approached.

She waved the shotgun at Caz. 'I caught this woman snooping around the place.'

'It's okay, love,' I reassured her, 'this is Caz. Annie and I met her earlier.'

'What the bloody hell is going on?' Caz said with panic in her voice. She backed away slowly with her hands up at waist height, her eyes wide with fear.

'I'm really sorry, Caz. We've had some issues with Caitlin's ex-partner. It's made us all very paranoid.' Then I turned to Caitlin. 'Maybe you should put the gun down, love.'

'Oh yes ... I'm so sorry,' she said to Caz.

'Jack!' I snapped my fingers and he came immediately to my side and sat down.

Caitlin looked embarrassed as she pointed over to the farmhouse. 'I'm just going to check on Mum.' She glanced at Caz who was still trying to calm down and get her breath. 'Once again, I am really sorry.'

Caz gave a sigh of relief. 'It's fine ... I should have explained myself a bit better.'

'Were you looking for me?' I asked.

'Yes. My house is only a mile away and I knew that you lived up here.'

'How can I help?'

'Mum told me about some of the things that you were asking her about to do with my sister's death. And Andrew Burrows and Sarah Meadows. There is something that she didn't tell you. Something from the past that might help you.'

I gestured over to the farmhouse. 'Why don't you come in?'

HAVING PLACED mugs on our kitchen table, I took over the freshly made pot of tea and a small jug of milk.

'Thank you,' Caz said quietly as she glanced between me and Annie. 'I went to see Louise earlier. At the hospital.'

'Yes,' I said with an empathetic expression.

'It's strange, because I've heard that when you see people like that they look like they're asleep,' she said softly, 'but Louise didn't look like she was sleeping. I don't know what it was, but I could tell that she was gone. She just wasn't there anymore. I don't know if that makes any sense?'

'It makes perfect sense,' Annie said gently as she started to pour the tea for everyone. 'I lost my sister very suddenly just over six months ago. When I went to see her, I thought exactly the same thing.'

'Did you?' Caz seemed relieved that someone else had the same feeling and thoughts as her.

Annie passed a cup of tea to her. 'Yes, I honestly did.'

'Thank you.'

There was a poignant silence.

I looked over at Caz. 'You said there was something from the past that you thought might be relevant to your sister's death. And the others.'

She nodded as she sipped her tea. 'Yes, that's right. To be honest, I don't know how relevant it is. But it's been on my mind since you talked to Mum earlier. You asked her about Andrew, Sarah and Louise at school.'

'That's right.'

'Well, they were all great friends at that time. I was three years below them so I remember. They were in Year 10, so I'm guessing they were all about fourteen. There was an accident at Llanfair slate mines in the summer holidays. A kid called Callum Jones was killed.'

Annie leaned forward over the table. 'What happened?'

'Louise said that a gang of them had all gone up to the mines to have a party. They were messing around - drinking and smoking weed and stuff like that. Callum ended up falling down a disused mine shaft and he was killed.'

'By accident?' I asked.

'No one seems to know. Some people said he'd just

tripped. Others said that someone had pushed him on purpose. The police were involved obviously.'

'Any idea if they suspected anyone of pushing him?' Annie asked.

'Louise wouldn't say, in fact she refused to talk about it. And that's when the friendship group split up. After that, none of them really spoke to each other again. I'm not sure why, or what happened. I guess the trauma of it was too much for them.'

I thought for a second. 'Do you know Judy Thompson?'

'The GP?' she asked.

'Yes. It's just that she was in the same year as all those people at the school, wasn't she?'

'Oh yes,' she said knowingly.

What's that about?

I picked up on it. 'Was she involved in what happened at the slate mine?'

'Involved? You're joking, aren't you?'

'What do you mean?'

'Judy was caught up right in the middle of it all,' Caz said. 'Or Bronwen, as she was known then.'

I was confused. 'Bronwen?'

'Her name was Bronwen Thompson. Bronwen Judith Thompson. When she came back from uni and medical school, she'd gone all la-de-da and changed her name to Judy.'

'And when you said that she was right in the middle of it all, what exactly did you mean?' I asked, wondering if we'd stumbled on something that was very relevant to the shootings.

'I'm not sure how she was involved, but she was arrested by the police and questioned about Callum's death. Someone told me that she had been arrested for manslaughter. Then she just disappeared. Someone said she'd been moved to another care home.'

'She was in care?' Annie asked.

'Yes. I think she got bullied quite a lot because of that. I remember her being a bit of an oddball, so you can imagine my surprise when she became the new GP just over a year ago.'

I shot a look over at Annie. No wonder Judy Thompson had seemed so uncomfortable when we'd asked about her time at school and her friendships with Andrew, Sarah and Louise.

Chapter 40

Annie and I had left the farmhouse and headed straight back to the medical centre. I wanted to confront Judy carefully with what Caz had told us, and ask her why she had lied so much. Was the accident at the slate mine the key to the shootings? There were far too many coincidences for it not to be.

As we came over the crest of the hill that led down to Dolgellau, the spring sunshine glinted off the dark tiles of the roofs in the distance. Beyond that was a series of low hills covered in grass. Behind them, the dark ominous shapes of the mountains of Eryri/Snowdonia.

'It just doesn't make any sense that Judy would lie to us so much,' Annie said, thinking out loud.

'Well it could be that she found it a very difficult time in her life,' I said, playing devil's advocate just for a moment. 'Maybe she just wasn't comfortable talking about it.'

'Then why didn't she just say that?' Annie gave me a dubious frown. 'She could have said that she didn't want to discuss it. Instead, she told us a pack of lies. I think it's very suspicious.'

'I agree,' I conceded. 'She's even changed the name that she uses.'

Annie then pointed to her phone. She had been trawling the internet to see if she could find anything out about the death of Callum Jones back in 2002.

'What is it?' I asked as we reached the middle of Dolgellau and I slowed down.

'Bronwen Thompson was charged with the manslaughter of Callum Jones in 2002,' she explained. 'It's strange because I don't remember the case. But it didn't go to trial.'

'Why not?' I asked.

'The Crown Prosecution Service said that there wasn't sufficient evidence,' Annie said as she continued to read from her screen, 'and all charges against her were dropped.'

My brain was whirring as I tried to make sense of this. I scratched at my beard.

'Maybe being accused of manslaughter ruined her life?' I said thoughtfully.

'And she blamed everyone who she was with that day for what had happened to her,' Annie said as we tried to put the pieces together and find a viable motive. 'So, she decided to start and take her revenge on them. After all, we know that she only arrived back in Dolgellau a year ago.'

I put my indicator on and turned left into the medical centre car park. 'And she's spent that time planning and making sure she knows where everyone is before she strikes.'

Annie pulled a face. 'Oh God. Does that seem far-fetched?'

'I'm just not sure. My instinct so far has been that Judy

DEADLY CARE

had nothing to do with the murders, but after she lied to us, and we've talked all this through, I'm starting to think it could be her.'

I pulled into a parking space and turned off the ignition. Then we both sat there for a few seconds as we tried to collect our thoughts.

Out of the corner of my eye, I saw a woman come out of the main entrance with a smart leather bag over her shoulder.

It was Judy.

'There she is,' I said quietly as I watched her.

Then I realised that she wasn't walking properly.

In fact, she was hobbling slightly as if she'd injured an ankle.

I narrowed my eyes. 'She's limping,' I whispered, as if to myself. It felt very important.

Annie's eyes widened with the significance of that fact. 'Didn't you say that the person you'd chased at the school had injured themselves jumping down from the fence?'

I nodded as I took a breath. 'Yes. I'm pretty sure they twisted their ankle.'

We watched Judy walk over to her car. The limp wasn't pronounced, but it was there all right.

Annie glanced out of the windscreen and then reached over and tapped my arm.

'What is it?' I asked, wondering what she'd spotted.

'Look at her keys,' she whispered.

I furrowed my brow. I had no idea what she was referring to so I shook my head.

'She's holding them in her left hand!'

My eyes widened.

Okay, this is more than suspicious.

'Do we confront her now?' Annie asked.

'No, I think we follow her and see where she's going.

For starters, I want to make sure that if she's responsible, she's not off to take her revenge on anyone else.'

'Oh God, of course.'

I started up the engine, and as Judy pulled away in her white Audi A3, I moved my truck slowly so that we were following her.

I concentrated on not making it obvious that we were behind her. 'Problem is, if she really is the killer, then she tried to run us off the road and she knows exactly what car we'll be in.'

Judy turned right and pulled away up the hill.

I followed slowly.

My eyes were straining to see her rear view mirror. It was a technique I'd picked up when working surveillance in CID. In the old days, we'd use two cars to tail a suspect for a major crime investigation like this. And as soon as I saw the suspect clocking me and my vehicle behind, I'd pull off into a side road and let the other surveillance team vehicle take over. And so on. Unfortunately, we didn't have that luxury today.

We reached a T-junction and Judy indicated to turn right.

As far as I could tell, she hadn't spotted us behind. Or maybe she was just doing a good job of hiding it.

There was a small gap in the traffic.

She pulled out quickly and sped away.

'Shit,' I muttered as I looked right and left. There were too many cars for me to safely pull out to follow her.

'Come on, come on,' Annie groaned in frustration.

The seconds ticked away agonisingly.

Finally, a gap appeared and I slammed my foot down on the accelerator.

We lurched forward and turned right.

As we hurtled around the bend, I could see the road stretching out for a mile or two infront of us.

Up ahead, an articulated lorry and a caravan were plodding on slowly.

I glanced over at Annie and shook my head.

We'd lost Judy. I just hoped that it didn't turn out to be a catastrophic mistake.

Now we needed to bring the police up to speed with what we'd discovered.

Chapter 41

Annie and I were sitting on a small but comfortable sofa in a side office next to CID at Dolgellau Police Station. It was usually an office reserved for whichever detective inspector was attached to CID but, as far as I knew, there were no DIs at Dolgellau. Dewi had his own separate office further along the corridor, but of course he was elsewhere at the moment.

'It's a while since I've been in here,' I said as I looked around the office. 'DI Charlie Winters was in here the last time I came but that was …,' I pulled a face when I realised how long ago it had been, '… about seventeen years ago. Bloody hell.'

We'd made ourselves known when we'd arrived at Dolgellau nick, and a very polite young DC had asked us to wait for Kelly and Ian in here. Glancing outside, I could see that the rest of the CID team were hard at work at computers or on the phone. I assumed there were another half a dozen out there following up on leads. To call what had happened in the past few days a major case was an understatement. I wondered if they'd make the decision to draft in officers from other areas to help out.

'Here we go,' Annie said as she shifted in her seat.

Kelly and Ian came in and sat on the two office chairs that were beside the desk.

'We got a call to say that you've got something for us and it's very urgent?' Kelly said as she sat forward on the chair.

Annie nodded. 'You could say that.'

I wasn't quite sure where to start. 'Caz Dyer came to see us. She told us that all the victims were caught up in an accident at the Llanfair slate mines in August 2002.'

Ian rested his forearms on the desk. 'Yes, I remember that. Callum Jones was the kid who was killed.'

Kelly raised an eyebrow. 'Yes, of course. I remember that our head teacher had to hold an assembly to tell us all what had happened.'

'Apparently, some kids were messing around in the slate mines and having a party. Drinking and smoking weed,' I explained. 'Something happened, and this boy named Callum Jones died.'

'And all three victims were there that day?' Kelly asked.

'Yes.'

She groaned in frustration. 'I can't believe that it's taken us this long to figure that out.'

Ian narrowed his eyes. 'And you think the murders are linked to that accident?'

'Possibly. There is something else,' I said with a darker expression. 'A girl called Bronwen Thompson was accused of being involved with Callum's death. She was arrested for his manslaughter.'

Ian looked over at us. 'Any idea where this Bronwen Thompson is now?'

'The GP at the Dolgellau Medical Centre who goes by

the name of Judy Thompson … is Bronwen Thompson,' I said. 'Her middle name is Judith.'

'What?' Kelly looked aghast and shook her head in disbelief.

'Wow,' Ian said under his breath. 'If I remember correctly, she was never charged or convicted of anything. Is that right?'

'Correct. CPS dropped all charges.'

'But why has she never mentioned any of this?' Kelly asked with a furrowed brow. 'We've spoken to her on numerous occasions and she's acted as if she doesn't know any of this.'

'We've no idea,' Annie replied, 'but we spoke to her earlier today. Not only did she fail to mention it, she also actively lied about her friendship with the victims.'

Ian raised an eyebrow. 'That's very suspicious, isn't it?'

'There's something else,' I added. 'We travelled back to the medical centre to confront her. However, we spotted her coming out, and she left the centre in her car. Not only was she walking with a slight limp, it looked like she might be left handed.'

'Jesus.' Kelly got up and went over to the computer.

Ian sighed. 'Crikey, it's got to be her, hasn't it?'

Kelly turned to look at him. 'We need to arrest her right now and bring her in. If it's her, we need to make sure she's not about to kill anyone else.'

'We tried to follow her out of Dolgellau for that very reason, but unfortunately we lost her.'

'We can use the local ANPR and see if we can get a hit,' Ian said to Kelly as he got up. 'Let me go and ring traffic. I'll make sure that all patrols are given her vehicle details and registration.'

'Thanks, Ian,' Kelly said. He left the room as she started to tap at the computer. 'I'm just taking a look at the

PNC and HOLMES to see if there are any notes for a Bronwen Thompson going back to the 90s.'

'Good idea,' I said as I watched her. She was pulling a face as she read from the screen. Whatever it was, it seemed to be very significant.

Then she looked over at Annie and I and gave us a dark look.

'According to the notes on the PNC, Bronwen Thompson was asked to leave the local care home she was living in in Dolgellau after several incidents. I haven't got any details, but local police officers were called out. In September 2002, she was moved to a care home down in Shropshire. In 2003, she was sexually assaulted and raped by two older boys in that home who were convicted and sent to prison.'

'Jesus,' I said under my breath.

'From 2003, she has a string of petty convictions. Assault, theft, drunk and disorderly,' Kelly continued, 'and then in 2006 that all stopped and there's nothing else on her record since.'

Annie frowned. 'She would have been seventeen or eighteen in 2006. If she trained to be a doctor, she must have knuckled down and turned her life round after that point.'

'Looks like it, but she must have still carried the trauma of the rape,' Kelly suggested. 'She might have blamed her friends from Dolgellau for what happened to her and Callum Jones. If that led to her being moved to another care home where she was attacked, possibly she thinks that's their fault?'

I nodded. 'If that's how she was thinking, then that definitely provides her with a strong motive for murder.'

'Now we just need to find her,' Annie said.

Chapter 42

Annie and I were heading out of Dolgellau along Arran Road. My head was whirling with the developments of the last two hours. My main concern was that Judy Thompson seemed intent on murdering anyone who'd been involved in the events at the Llanfair slate mine in August 2002 where Callum Jones had met his death. We needed to somehow find anyone else who had been there that day before they were murdered too.

Annie was busy typing away on her phone. 'I think I've got something here. The newspaper reports at the time of Callum's death mention some of the kids who were arrested by the police. The name Cathy Reeves comes up several times. And I've got a Cathy Reeves, Yoga and Pilates Teacher, who lives in Minffordd.'

Minffordd – meaning *Roadside* in Welsh – was a village that was located between Porthmadog and Penrhyndeudraeth.

'Better go and see if we can find her then,' I said as I started to plan the quickest route.

'Hold on,' Annie said abruptly.

I glanced over and saw that she was staring out at an Audi garage over to our right.

'What is it?' I said, slowing the truck.

'I think I saw Judy Thompson's car in the car park back there.'

'Okay.' I checked my mirrors, slowed, and then did a U-turn.

The Audi garage was now on our left-hand side.

As I crawled past at about 5mph I scanned the customer car park.

Then I spotted a white Audi A3.

It was Judy Thompson's car. I recognised the number plate.

'Yes, that's definitely her car,' I said quietly as I indicated and pulled into the car park.

Annie was already making a phone call. She put her phone on speaker.

Kelly answered. 'DS Taylor, Dolgellau CID.'

'Kelly? It's Annie,' she said with a sense of urgency. 'We've just pulled into the Audi garage on Arran Road. Judy Thompson's car is in the customer car park.'

'Is she definitely there?'

'We don't know yet,' Annie replied.

'Okay. We're on our way. If she's there do not approach her. She might have a gun.'

'All right,' Annie said and ended the call.

I turned to her. 'I'm not sitting here twiddling my thumbs. Judy might be in there planning on killing someone else.'

Annie nodded in agreement. 'Okay, but let's just take it nice and easy, eh? I'd prefer not to get shot today.'

'I wish my shotgun wasn't at home,' I said in frustration.

'Yes, well it might be a good thing that it is, Clint,' she said dryly as we got out.

I looked towards the building straight in front of us.

There were large glass doors with a big sign above that read *Audi – Dolgellau,* along with a phone number and website address.

The word *RECEPTION* was painted in block capitals on the ground in front of the doors, along with another sign that read *Croeso – Welcome.*

My pulse had now quickened.

On the one hand, given that Judy owned an Audi, her visit to the garage might be nothing more sinister than booking a service or buying new parts. However, given her pattern of behaviour in recent days, I knew we had to be very careful as she might be hunting down another victim. And she would be armed.

Moving cautiously towards the double doors, I saw that Judy was inside and sitting at a desk opposite a young man. They were in conversation, and the man was looking at his computer monitor. It seemed relatively innocuous.

I glanced at Annie. 'Doesn't look like she's doing anything more than booking in a service.'

'No,' she agreed, 'but let's not get lulled into a false sense of security.'

We watched as Judy got up from the desk, turned, and started to walk towards the doors.

Before Annie and I had time to react or move out of sight, she had started to open one of the doors and had spotted us.

'Hi Judy,' I said calmly, wondering how we were going to explain this 'coincidence'.

'Hi,' she said suspiciously.

Annie pointed inside to the showroom. 'I'm shopping for a new car.'

DEADLY CARE

'Oh, I love my Audi,' Judy said. 'I can highly recommend them. It's my third.'

'Good to know.'

'I'm sorry if I was a bit evasive earlier,' she said while pulling an apologetic face. 'Lot on my mind. Nice to see you.'

She took a step to pass us.

I could hear the sound of sirens approaching.

'It's okay,' I said. 'We know about what happened at the Llanfair slate mine and Callum Jones' death.'

She stopped in her tracks.

The blood visibly drained from her face. 'What?'

The sirens were now deafening as two police cars screeched into the car park behind us, blue lights flashing.

Judy narrowed her eyes. 'What the hell is going on?'

'And we know what happened to you at the care home in Shropshire,' Annie announced.

Judy gritted her teeth. 'That's none of your business,' she snapped.

Then she locked eyes with me as her left hand moved towards her large handbag.

Oh shit!

I tensed as I prepared to launch myself at her.

'Armed police!' yelled a male voice from behind me. 'Put both your hands where I can see them - now!'

Annie and I moved back slowly.

An authorised firearms officer – AFO – wearing a black Kevlar bulletproof vest and holding a Glock 19 handgun appeared.

'Don't move!' he barked.

Judy took a step backwards and put her hands up waist height. 'I don't know what's going on, but this is a big mistake.'

Kelly and Ian looked at me as they approached.

'Judith Thompson,' Kelly said as she flashed her warrant card. 'I'm arresting you on suspicion of murder. You do not have to say anything, but anything you do say can be used as evidence in a court of law.'

Judy took another step back. 'This is bloody ridiculous!'

'Please stay where you are,' the AFO said sternly.

Ian pulled out a pair of handcuffs and took a step forward to cuff her.

Instinctively, she moved backwards across the verge and then onto the road.

'Watch out!' Annie yelled.

I watched in horror as a small white van ploughed straight into Judy, knocking her up into the air.

A second later, she crashed onto the road and lay motionless.

'Oh my God,' Annie gasped.

Chapter 43

I looked up and saw Annie coming along the hospital corridor with two coffees. We'd decided to follow the ambulance, and Kelly and Ian, up to Glan Clwyd Hospital. After the accident, I'd gone to check on Judy before the paramedics had arrived. She was breathing and had a pulse, but it was clear that she'd been severely injured.

'Here you go,' Annie said, still walking with some difficulty.

'I don't know why you didn't let me go and get these,' I said, shaking my head.

'Because if I don't keep moving, this bloody knee starts to seize up,' she said in a withering tone as she sat down next to me and handed me my coffee. 'And I don't know how you can drink that stuff black with no sugar.' She pointed to her own coffee. 'I need at least two spoonsful to make it palatable.'

I rolled my eyes. 'This coming from the woman who won't have bloody biscuits in her house.'

Annie ignored me and gestured down the corridor towards the entrance to the Intensive Care and Major

Trauma Unit. It had been about twenty minutes since Kelly and Ian had disappeared inside.

'I'm surprised she actually survived that accident,' Annie said as she sipped her coffee.

I nodded in agreement. 'We have to hope she pulls through. The relatives of Andrew, Sarah, and Louise deserve justice. She needs to stand trial for what she's done. If she dies in there, that won't happen.'

'True,' Annie said, 'but I guess there might be some relatives who won't be that upset if she dies.'

I saw the doors to the ICU opening, and Kelly and Ian came out. They were talking intently as they got closer.

'What's the latest?' I asked quietly.

'They've had to put her into an induced coma,' Ian informed us. 'CT scan revealed a fractured skull with a possible bleed on the brain.'

Kelly looked at us. 'She's critical but stable. Fingers crossed that she makes it through the night.'

'What about her bag?' I asked.

Kelly had taken her bag from the road and asked forensics to examine it.

'No firearm inside,' she said.

I frowned. I was convinced that Judy was reaching inside the bag for a gun when the police had arrived.

Chapter 44

It was starting to get dark by the time I wandered down from the farmhouse with two beers. I'd dropped Annie home as she had a few things to do. My plan was to take Caitlin and Sam back over to her house later.

As I walked towards the paddock, Jack padded alongside me. I took in the apricot colour of the sky as the sun slumped slowly over the uneven ridges of Eryri/Snowdonia's mountains. There was a stretched ribbon of thin cloud that had started to tinge with the faintest hint of magenta. The air smelled of blossom, and the natural earth aroma that came over from the paddock where Sam was riding.

'These are the last two beers,' I said as I handed one to Caitlin, 'unless you want a can of Old Speckled Hen bitter next?'

She pulled a face. 'Ew. The last time I took a sip of your pint of bitter it tasted like warm mud.'

I laughed. 'And how old were you when you did that?'

'About eight.' She reached down and stroked the top of

Jack's head. 'We've always had German Shepherds, haven't we?'

I nodded. 'We've had four since we moved in. Such a lovely breed. They used to have a terrible reputation. I don't know why. If they're trained properly, they're fantastic dogs.'

'I remember there was Leo. Then Hank …'

'And Bruno,' I reminded her.

She sighed deeply. 'Oh yes, Bruno. But Jack is definitely my favourite.'

'Lechyd Da,' I said as I clinked her bottle.

'Lechyd Da,' she said, raising her bottle before taking a long swig.

'He's doing all right, isn't he?' I said, gesturing to Sam who was trotting around the paddock on Lleuad.

Caitlin nodded and gave me a meaningful look.

'What?' I asked.

'You know what he said to me last night?' she said quietly.

I shook my head. 'No.'

'He said he wished he'd been born here and grown up here all his life because it makes him so happy,' she gushed. 'And that I was so lucky to have a dad like you. I wanted to cry.' Then she gave me a cheeky grin. 'Of course, I didn't tell him what you're really like.'

'Ha ha.' I rolled my eyes.

'Sounds like you and Annie have had quite a day of it,' she said. 'It was all over the news at lunchtime.'

I nodded. 'I'm glad that Judy Thompson is where she is now and can't harm anyone else.'

'Any idea if she'll live?'

'No, but I hope she does for obvious reasons.'

'Yeah, of course.'

Caitlin was smart enough to understand.

DEADLY CARE

'All three victims were in Year 7 just as I was leaving sixth form,' she pointed out. 'It's dreadful to think that they've gone.'

I raised an eyebrow. 'Did you know any of them?'

'No, not really ... I think that Louise Dyer sometimes came to the Dolgellau Youth Centre when I used to help run that. At least I think it was her.'

'Oh yes. I forgot you used to help out down there,' I said. It seemed like a lifetime ago.

She narrowed her eyes. 'Horrible thing is that I do remember Callum Jones and his brother Stu. They came down to play table tennis a couple of times. Callum was this tiny little thing, and his brother was very protective of him.'

I nodded, but my eye had been caught by something glinting in the woods over to our right. It was where I'd seen and chased Dean Ashgrove two days ago.

'What is it?' Caitlin asked.

'I'm not sure,' I said quietly and passed her my beer. 'Hold this.'

'Dad, you're scaring me.'

My eyes were locked onto the woods. There was a glint of something again. It didn't look metallic. More like glass.

Binoculars.

Someone was watching us from the woods.

'Fuckers,' I growled as I stormed up the pathway full of rage.

Opening the front door, I saw that Caitlin's shotgun was propped up against the wall. I would have preferred my Winchester but this would have to do.

Clicking it open, I saw that it was loaded with two red cartridges.

As I turned to come down the path again, Caitlin was coming towards me.

'Dad, you need to tell me what's going on,' she said, looking anxious.

'I think there's someone watching us from the woods over there,' I said, gesturing.

She looked aghast. 'But you can't just go and shoot them!'

'Watch me.'

'Dad!'

'It'll be a warning shot,' I reassured her. I was so angry that I wasn't thinking straight.

I marched across the front of the farmhouse, down and over the dry stone wall, and into the field.

The woods were about forty yards away.

Someone was definitely moving around in there. The undergrowth was being disturbed.

Striding across the field towards the trees, I pulled up the shotgun, nestled it into the crook of my shoulder, and stopped.

Closing one eye, I scanned the woods again, waiting for another sign of movement.

Even though I was tempted to fire directly at whoever was in there, I wasn't about to risk a charge of manslaughter.

I saw a figure moving past a tree but I couldn't make out anything more than their shape.

Aiming the gun into the branches above them, I squeezed the trigger.

CRACK!

A small sprinkling of leaves and twigs fell from the tree where it had been ripped apart by the gunshot.

'OH MY GOD!' shouted a man's terrified voice.

The next thing, two men in their 60s came charging out of the woods with their hands up as if they were in a film.

DEADLY CARE

'Don't shoot, don't shoot!' one of them with a beard shouted, clearly terrified.

They both wore hiking gear, and had binoculars hanging from straps around their necks.

Jesus Christ!

I gave a frustrated snort as I lowered the shotgun and stormed towards them.

'What the bloody hell are you doing in there?' I thundered angrily.

'We've … heard that .. that there was a very rare sighting of a roseate tern in these woods,' the other man stammered nervously.

'What the bloody hell is a roseate tern?' I demanded.

'It's one of the rarest UK breeding birds,' he explained, as if it was a stupid question.

I took a long breath. 'Sorry. I thought you were in there spying on us!'

'Spying on you?' the man asked with a frown.

I put the shotgun down to my side.

'Sorry if I scared you,' I said grumpily, and then turned to walk back to the farmhouse leaving the two twitchers to find their roseate tern!

Chapter 45

I pulled out a heavy whiskey glass from the cupboard. Then I went over to the little drinks cabinet, reached inside, and took my bottle of Jameson's. There was always something reassuring about the dark green glass of the bottle. It was a whiskey that had been distilled in Dublin since the late 1700s, and that kind of history felt comforting. Opening the freezer, I reached inside and plucked a large ice cube from the tray. Then I dropped the ice cube from about three inches into the glass so that it made a little plonking sound. I unscrewed the top of the Jameson's and poured in two fingers of the whiskey. The ice made a tiny cracking noise. Taking the glass in the palm of my hand, I swirled the ice cube and golden liquid around about half a dozen times. And then finally I lifted it to my lips, and let the thick, earthy aroma drift up into my nostrils before taking a sip. What I loved was the ritual of all this. Taking the time to slow down, relax, and be mindful for a few seconds.

Letting out an audible sigh, I took a step towards the door when my phone rang.

It was Ethan.

'Hi Ethan.'

'Hey, Frank,' he said in his usual friendly, upbeat tone.

'I'm glad you called,' I said. 'I need a favour. If I text you over Judy Thompson's number plate, can you check her movements in the past few days on the North Wales ANPR for us?'

'No problem, Frank. I'll give it a go.'

'Everything else okay?' I asked. It was unusual for him to call me, especially during the evening.

'I think I have some good news for you,' he said. 'I've managed to get a hit on that transit van that you asked me to check out.'

He was referring to the van that Dean Ashcroft had been driving when I'd chased him out of the woods.

'Great. Where did you get the hit?' I asked.

'Watford,' he replied.

Watford?

'I'll send it over for you to look at, but there's a guy in it that I assume is this TJ chap. Looks like he's moving into a flat.'

I took a few seconds to process this. If Ethan was right, this could be the news that we had been waiting for. But I didn't want to get my hopes up.

'I'll fire it over as an MP4 file and you can have a watch.'

'Thank you, Ethan,' I said gratefully. 'This means a lot to us.'

'No problem. Glad to be of service,' he said. 'Speak soon.'

He ended the call and I immediately headed for my study to grab my laptop. I then brought it back to the table, opened it up, and went into my emails. The video file had just arrived. I double-clicked on it and then waited for it to open.

Sipping at my whiskey, I watched as my laptop screen went black. After a few seconds, the footage from an ANPR camera appeared.

It began with a view of a Clarendon Road in Watford. Yesterday's date was on the timecode.

Dean Ashton's white transit van came into shot, parked up on the pavement, and its hazard lights started to flash.

Two figures got out. They were wearing baseball caps, but it was clearly Dean Ashcroft and TJ.

TJ went over to a building, jogged up the steps, took out some keys, and then opened the front door. He then went back to the van where Dean had opened the back doors.

For the next two minutes I watched as they ferried bags, a suitcase, and a few boxes from the van into what I assumed was a flat.

For whatever reason, TJ had decided to head back to London for now.

The sense of relief was overwhelming.

Jumping up, I popped in to see Rachel who was fast asleep in front of the news on the telly.

Then I made my way out of the farmhouse and headed for the annexe.

The front door opened and Caitlin and Sam came out. They were clearly about to head over to Annie's for the night.

'Hey,' I said in a cheery voice.

Sam smiled and gave a little wave. 'Hi Taid.'

I looked at Caitlin. 'It's okay. You don't need to go to Annie's tonight. Or again, actually.'

She raised an eyebrow quizzically. 'What are you talking about, Dad?'

I gestured to the annexe. 'Let's go inside and I can explain.'

We all turned and headed back through the front door.

Chapter 46

Rachel giggled as she sat back in her reclining chair. 'A roseate tern?'

'I know,' I said, shaking my head. 'A bloody roseate tern.'

I was watching the telly with Rachel and recounting my conversation with the two birdwatchers from earlier.

'And you shot at them, Frank?' she asked, her eyes twinkling with amusement.

'I wouldn't say that I shot at them.'

She chortled. 'Well, that's what Caitlin told me.'

'It was more of a warning shot to frighten them off,' I admitted.

'It sounds like you did more than frighten them,' Rachel said. 'I'm surprised that one of them didn't have a heart attack!'

'Oh well.' I shrugged and then pointed over to the plate of hobnobs that I'd brought in about ten minutes ago with a mug of tea. 'You haven't touched your biscuits yet.'

'Oh gosh. I forgot they were there,' she said.

I sat back and took a deep breath.

Not only were TJ and Dean Ashcroft now down in Watford, Judy Thompson was lying in a coma in hospital.

For the first time in a long time, I actually felt relaxed and had a clear head.

Rachel roared with laughter at something on the television.

I watched her for a few seconds, smiled to myself, and gave an audible sigh.

This all feels better now, doesn't it?

I was hoping that life would be less eventful from now on.

Chapter 47

Annie had been sitting on Meredith's bed for about half an hour. They'd been chatting and laughing as Annie filled Meredith in on the extraordinary events of the last few days.

Meredith sighed, shaking her head in disbelief. 'Haven't you and Frank thought of taking up something a little less stressful like bridge or golf?'

Ethan poked his head in and gave Annie a meaningful look. 'I might need to borrow you for a minute.'

'Okay,' she said with a frown. Whatever it was, his expression and tone seemed to suggest that it was serious.

'Put the kettle on while you're up, would you love?' Meredith said.

Annie nodded as she followed Ethan into the hallway. 'What's going on?' she asked him.

He gestured to his office. 'Something I need to show you.'

'Sounds ominous,' Annie said, pulling a face as she followed him into the room that was full of computers, monitors, and hard drive equipment.

'Unfortunately, it might be,' he admitted as he sat down in his large, padded computer chair. He sat forward and started to type, and Annie settled herself on the plastic chair beside him.

'What is it?' she asked, now starting to worry.

'Frank asked me to hack into the North Wales ANPR to track down the van that he chased the other day.'

'Yes, I know about that.'

'He also asked me to feed in the licence plate of an Audi A3 registered to Judy Thompson,' he said as he turned to look at her. 'She's the woman you think carried out these murders in Dolgellau, isn't she?'

Annie nodded, but she didn't like where Ethan was going with this. 'We're 99% sure. Why?'

'I worked backwards through the shootings. So, the shooting at Ysgol y Mynydd happened at around 8.30am yesterday as stated by media sources.'

'According to Frank, that sounds about right,' Annie agreed.

Ethan pointed to the large monitor infront of him. 'Well the problem is … this is Judy Thompson's Audi A3 coming past an ANPR camera on the A470 into Dolgellau at 8.34am,' he said. He froze the ANPR footage to show the Audi.

'Shit,' Annie muttered under her breath, 'that's not good.'

Ethan shrugged. 'And she can't be in two places at once.'

'No, she can't.' Annie moved forward on her seat and peered carefully at the screen. 'Can you see that it's actually Judy Thompson driving that car?'

He tapped at the computer to enlarge the image. However, the pixelation was too severe and there was no way of seeing the driver. 'Unfortunately not.'

'So, I backtracked to the shooting of the paramedic ... Sarah Meadows. That happened two days ago at about 3.15pm.'

'Okay.' Annie was feeling confused and concerned. Had they all got it wrong about Judy Thompson's guilt? Everything pointed towards her.

'Then I did some digging around in the main UK Audi database,' Ethan explained. 'I hacked into their GPS tracking centre.'

Annie narrowed her eyes. 'Their what?' She roughly knew what GPS was but it needed explaining.

'All new cars, or at least all new prestige cars like an Audi,' Ethan said, 'have a GPS tracker attached to the car. And unless the owner deliberately turns it off, that vehicle can be tracked via the installed GPS. All you need is the code of the specific tracker.'

'Which you found?' Annie asked.

'Naturally.'

'And?'

'Thing is, Judy Thompson's Audi was parked up in central Dolgellau at the time of Sarah Meadow's shooting. She arrived in the town sometime after 2pm and then left again at 3.47pm. Of course, she could have been visiting a patient or doing her shopping.'

'Or preparing to ambush and shoot Sarah Meadows,' Annie suggested.

'Exactly. And we don't know that she was even driving her car when the ANPR clocked it yesterday,' Ethan pointed out.

'That's very confusing. What about when Andrew Burrows was shot?' Annie asked. She knew that the killer had been driving a silver VW Golf which they had dumped and torched over in Coed y Brenin Park. Then there was the sighting of a ginger-haired woman acting strangely and then leaving in a hurry in a dark BMW. None of that fitted Judy Thompson. However, the woman in the park might have no connection at all to the person who dumped and torched the VW Golf.

Ethan shook his head. 'Her Audi was parked at the medical centre for most of the day, but that doesn't mean that <u>she</u> was there the whole day. There's something else,' he said. 'What if Judy Thompson isn't working alone? If there are two killers, that could explain the discrepancies.'

Annie sighed. It was a possibility that neither she or Frank had even considered yet.

Chapter 48

It was the following morning, and Annie and I were now back in the DI's office in Dolgellau CID. We felt it was vital that we show Kelly and Ian what Ethan had discovered. Annie had sent the ANPR file over to Kelly at 6am to see if she could get the digital forensics team to enhance the image.

'Right, I've got the footage back.' She turned the monitor to show Annie and I. 'Not good news,' she said as she pointed to the image on the screen. It definitely showed Judy Thompson at the wheel of her Audi. 'Judy Thompson is travelling along this road at the exact time that Louise Dyer was shot dead,' she said with an exasperated sigh.

Ian raised his shoulders. 'It means that she couldn't have done it. And that calls into question whether she was responsible for the other murders too.'

Annie frowned. 'It doesn't make any sense,' she groaned with a perturbed expression. 'I thought that everything fitted together. Judy was at the slate mine that day with all of our victims. The fact that she was arrested for

Callum's murder seems to have set off a course of events that ruined her life.'

'Unless she's doing this with someone else,' Kelly suggested.

There were a few seconds of silence.

'Or we've just got the wrong person,' I said.

There was a knock at the open door.

A female detective in her 40s looked in and gestured to Ian. 'Can I have a word?' she asked, implying it was significant.

'Of course,' he said, getting up from his seat. 'Won't be a minute.'

Kelly gave us a look as Ian talked outside. 'And I'm not going to ask you how you got this ANPR footage in the first place,' she said dryly.

'No comment,' I joked.

Ian marched back in with a quizzical look on his face as he sat down and glanced at us all. Whatever he'd learned, it seemed to be significant. 'I took down the VIN number of the Land Rover Defender that we found torched.' Then he looked at me. 'And this was the vehicle that rammed you off the road?'

I nodded to confirm this. 'Yes, that's right.'

'We're assuming that the killer was aware that you were digging around in these shootings and they wanted you out of the way,' Ian continued.

'That's what we have to assume,' Annie agreed.

He gestured to the piece of paper in his hand. 'Turns out the Land Rover Defender is registered to an Oliver Booth. We've got an address. A farm about ten miles north of here.'

Kelly looked mystified. 'And who is Oliver Booth?'

Ian gave us all a knowing look. 'I've no idea. But it

turns out that he was in that class of 2002 at Ysgol y Mynydd.'

'Really?' Kelly shrugged. 'I don't remember the name. But there's no way it's a coincidence. Let's go and see what he's got to say for himself, eh?'

Ian stood up and looked over at me. 'Wanna meet us there, Frank?'

I nodded. 'Sounds like a plan.'

Chapter 49

Half an hour later, Annie and I pulled in to the yard of Manor Farm which was located just south of Ffestiniog. However, the farm was completely deserted and derelict except for a battered maroon Volvo Estate car.

'Doesn't look like anyone lives here,' Annie said with a frown as we peered through the windscreen.

Jack gave a little whine and I stroked his head. 'It's all right, boy. You can get out and stretch your legs in a minute. Just need to check all this is okay.'

Annie opened the passenger door and got out. I followed, and scoured the large pot-holed yard and empty farm buildings. Over to our right was the farmhouse. It was totally dilapidated, with broken windows and tiles missing from the roof.

The wind picked up and whistled through the yard, sending a rusty old oil can skittering along the ground.

I had to admit I was a little spooked. It was hard to tell if anyone actually lived here.

I felt the buzz of my phone in my pocket. My immediate thought was that there might be a problem back at our farmhouse.

Checking it quickly, I saw that there was a missed call from the Dolgellau Leisure Centre.

'Everything okay?' Annie asked as she buttoned up her coat against the increasing wind.

'Missed call from the leisure centre.' I didn't know if it was significant, or just a call to say that they'd been unable to trace the person who had called in there earlier in the week. 'I'll ring back when we're finished here.'

We stood at the front of the truck and leaned against the bonnet. The wind swirled around the yard again and made a deep groaning sound as it swept through the towering feed shed to our far right.

Something on Annie's phone seemed to have captured her full attention. She looked perplexed.

'What's up?' I asked, noticing her changed expression.

'There's an article in one of the tabloids today about the shootings,' she said as she turned her phone to me. The screen showed a school photo with a caption that read *Upper School, Ysgol y Mynydd, Dolgellau, 2002*.

'You know the one person who hasn't come up in any of this?' she said, thinking out loud.

'No, I don't,' I admitted.

She pointed to the article on her phone. 'Stu Jones, Callum's older brother.'

I furrowed my brow. 'How do you mean?'

'Well, no one seems to know exactly what happened to Callum that day at the mine, but according to this article, he might have been pushed. Not only that, it also says that Stu Jones was holding on to his brother who was hanging down the mine shaft. He yelled for the others to help pull his brother up but they ran away, leaving Stu on his own.

Eventually he couldn't hold on to his brother any longer and had to let go.'

'Oh God, that's horrific.' I paused for a little while then had a sudden moment of clarity. 'So ... if anyone wanted to get their revenge on that group of friends, it would have been him, wouldn't it?'

'They abandoned him while he tried to save his brother. If they'd helped, Callum might have lived. It's obvious now that Stu Jones would blame them all for his brother's death,' Annie said, joining up the dots.

I gestured to her camera. 'Can I have another look at that school photo?'

'Of course,' she said as she turned the screen.

I leaned closer and peered at all the teenagers' faces. Even though they weren't named, I spotted Andrew Burrows immediately. Then Louise Dyer. Finally, Sarah Meadows. But no Judy Thompson.

'No Judy Thompson,' I said, gesturing to the screen.

'Maybe she wasn't at school that day?' Annie suggested.

'I wonder if Oliver Booth is in this photo?'

I glanced at my watch, wondering what was taking Kelly and Ian so long to get here.

Then out of the corner of my eye, I spotted something in the photo that jumped out at me.

A small teenage boy with distinctive sticking out ears.

Isn't that Ian Ramsey?

'Do you recognise that kid?' I asked, pointing to the photo.

Annie's eyes widened as she looked up at me. 'It looks remarkably like Ian Ramsey, doesn't it? Why is he in that photo?'

'I've no idea.' I felt my stomach lurch. What the hell was Ian doing in the photograph?

Then I had a thought and I quickly dialled Caitlin.

'Hi Dad,' she said brightly. 'Everything is okay here, don't worry.'

I sighed. 'Oh good. Actually, there's something that I need you to help me with and it's quite urgent. You said that you remembered some of the kids from school in 2002 when you were in Sixth Form there? The class where all the victims have come from?'

'I can't promise anything, but yes I do remember some of them,' she said. 'Why, what is it?'

'Can you get your phone, go onto *The Mirror Online*, and click on today's article about the victims of these shootings for me?'

'Of course ... Okay, I've got it.'

'Can you see the photo of the Upper School?' I asked.

'Yes, I can see that,' she replied.

'Front row, far left, there's a boy. He's quite small with sticking out ears. Can you see him?'

'Yes, I can see him.'

'We think that boy is DC Ian Ramsey who we've been working with,' I said. 'The only thing is that he hasn't mentioned his connection to this class, or the victims, which is incredibly suspicious.'

There was silence at the end of the phone.

'Caitlin?'

Nothing.

'Dad,' she said quietly, 'that boy isn't Ian Ramsey. It's Stu Jones, Callum's brother.'

What?

My whole body reacted. 'Jesus,' I gasped. 'Are you sure?'

'I'm positive. Are you okay, Dad?'

'Yes. I've got to go but I'm fine.' I ended the call and looked in astonishment at Annie.

'What? What is it, Frank? You're scaring me,' she said.

I took a breath to steady myself. 'Caitlin says that boy is Stu Jones.'

'Oh my God!' she exclaimed in shock. 'Who is Ian Ramsey then?'

'I suspect that Ian Ramsey doesn't exist,' I said as I called the number for the Dolgellau Leisure Centre.

'Doesn't exist?' Annie said under her breath.

'Hello, Leisure Centre,' said a young female voice.

I put the phone onto speaker so Annie could hear as well.

'Hi there. My name's Frank Marshal. You called me about fifteen minutes ago?'

'Oh yes,' she said. 'Well, Mr Marshal. I've got some good and bad news on trying to find the person who you think hit your friend's car.'

'Okay.'

'The bad news is that we couldn't find the person who came in that morning anywhere on our system, I'm afraid,' she said apologetically. 'We think that he didn't actually enter the leisure centre for some reason.'

'He?' I asked, picking up on her use of the word.

'He, yes. You see I asked around, and our delivery driver recognised the man who came in that morning. Said he hadn't seen him for ages.'

'What was his name?' I asked, holding my breath in anticipation.

'Stuart Jones,' she said nonchalantly. 'The driver said that his family moved away after his brother died in an accident.'

My head began to spin. 'Right, thank you.' I ended the call and looked at Annie.

'We got it very, very wrong,' she said in disbelief.

My brain was already leaping ahead. I looked around

at the deserted farm and remembered that it had been Ian who had told us to meet him here.

'I've got a nasty feeling that there is no Oliver Booth,' I said, giving Annie a dark look.

She narrowed her eyes. 'Ian set us up?'

I gestured to the truck. 'Maybe. Either way, I think we need to get out of here right now.'

Moving very quickly, Annie and I jumped into the truck and I started the ignition.

Slamming the Ranger into reverse, I backed up and turned the steering wheel hard left. As we straightened up, I pushed down hard on the accelerator.

We pulled out of the farmyard at speed. Jack gave a little whine as he sensed our unease.

Annie sighed. 'Close call, I think.'

As she spoke, my eyes were already locked on to a trail of dirt coming from the track further up.

Shit!

'Or maybe not,' I groaned.

Within seconds, a blue Astra was in front of us, blocking our path.

I slammed on the brakes as there was no room on the track to get past.

Ian jumped out of the car.

Looking right and left, I saw that there were dry stone walls on both sides of the track. Not even my truck was going to knock through those.

We were stuck.

'Bollocks,' I growled.

'Bollocks indeed,' Annie said under her breath. 'Now what?'

Ian approached the truck, pulled out a handgun, and pointed it at us through the windscreen.

'GET OUT OF THE CAR!' he yelled.

He was holding the gun in his left hand!

We both opened the doors slowly and got out.

Jack started to bark loudly.

'Leave the dog in there, or I'll shoot him!' Ian shouted, waving his gun. He looked anxious.

I clicked my fingers to get Jack's attention. He was snarling. He knew that something was wrong.

'Stay there, boy,' I commanded him.

'Close the doors!' Ian snapped.

'What's the plan, Stuart?' I asked. Annie slammed her door shut, and I pushed the driver's door so that it wasn't fully closed, in the hope that he wouldn't notice.

'You can't just shoot us,' Annie pleaded as she stood with her hands held up. 'This isn't going to bring Callum back, is it?'

'Shut up!' Ian gritted his teeth. 'Don't you dare talk about my brother,' he snarled.

'I get it. Those kids left you holding Callum,' I said, trying to placate him as much as I could. I was trying to buy time while I thought of a way of getting us out of this. 'If they'd helped you, poor Callum would be alive now, wouldn't he?'

'Yes, he would be.' Ian's face twisted with anger and pain. He lifted the gun and fired a shot over our heads. 'But I already warned you! I'm not here to talk about my brother. It's too late for that.'

'Why?' Annie asked in a gentle voice.

Ian turned his head slightly to look at Annie.

I used the chance to scour the ground by my feet.

A large grey rock, about the size of a grapefruit, lay in the grass nearby.

'From what I know, Callum was a lovely, gentle little

boy,' Annie said quietly. I didn't know if she was trying to upset Ian, but she was doing a good job. Maybe if he was rattled, he'd let his guard down.

'Be quiet!' he snapped.

I glanced down again at the rock. It was a long shot – literally!

Jack continued to bark and whine inside, but I knew he would stay in the truck until I commanded him otherwise.

'I can't believe that your parents would want you to be doing this,' Annie said, shaking her head.

'They're dead,' he replied, his voice filled with anger and resentment. He reached into his trouser pocket and pulled out a handful of black plastic ties.

'You don't need to do this,' Annie continued. 'What would Callum say if he knew you were doing all this in his name?'

Now completely enraged, he marched over towards Annie. 'You've gone too far now!' he screamed at her, waving the gun in her face.

Oh shit!

He was completely distracted.

Reaching down, I grabbed the rock and hurled it towards him.

It hit his neck and shoulder with a thud.

Then I grabbed the truck door, pulled it open, and clicked my fingers, gesturing for Jack to come out. 'Come on, boy!'

Before Ian had a chance to gather himself, Jack had sprinted over and knocked him to the ground while biting at his left hand.

He roared with pain. 'Ah, get off!' Blood was dripping from his forearm.

I ran over and kicked him as hard as I could in the side of the head.

He was instantly dazed and let go of the gun.

I reached down, grabbed the gun, and clicked my fingers again. 'Jack, come here boy!'

'Bloody hell!' Annie shrieked.

Ian was lying on his back holding his jaw where I'd kicked him.

I pointed the gun at his face. 'Do anything stupid and I'll shoot you. Roll over.'

'No chance,' he sneered.

I stepped forward, put my boot on his throat, and pointed the gun at his forehead. 'Roll over or I'm going to shoot you. And believe me, I really don't care.'

He groaned and rolled onto his front.

'Hands behind your back,' I snapped.

Then I knelt down, put my knee in the middle of his back, and pointed the gun to the back of his head.

Annie moved in, taking one of the plastic ties from the ground, and secured his hands.

It was only now that I could hear a metallic banging sound.

'What's that?' I said, looking at Annie.

It was coming from the Astra.

I moved towards the car and could hear the sound was coming from the boot.

Someone was inside it and banging.

Reaching down, I opened it and saw that it was Kelly inside. She was tied up and gagged.

Bloody hell.

I put the gun down, untied her, and pulled the gag from her mouth.

'Thank you,' she gasped.

I helped her out of the boot and she dusted herself down.

I picked up the gun and offered it to her. 'I guess I should give this to you?'

'Don't worry about that. You just saved my life, Frank.'

50

Five Days Later

With the sun starting to set behind us, Sam and I galloped across the open fields back towards the farmhouse. We'd been out for about two hours and I'd taken him cross-country to show him Maes Camlan, just south of Mawddwy. Legend had it that Maes Camlan – meaning *Field of Camlan* – was the location of King Arthur's final and fatal battle against his nephew, Mordred.

As we reached the dry stone walls that flanked our land we turned left towards the paddock. Outside the front of the farmhouse, Caitlin and Annie were sitting around a fire pit, blankets around their shoulders. Even though it had been a gloriously hot day, it was still April and the evenings could be very cold.

Getting down from Duke, I patted his sweaty flank. 'Thatta boy.' He whinnied and blew as I looked over at Sam who was getting down from Lleuad.

'You okay to take them down to the stables and make sure there's enough feed and water, mate?' I called over to him.

He gave me a grin and a thumbs up. 'No problem, Taid.'

I had a little smile to myself at my grandson's overwhelming enthusiasm for nearly everything.

Wandering slowly up the path, I gazed over to the setting sun that had painted the sky a fiery reddish pink. I hoped it meant that tomorrow would be another beautiful day.

'You were gone ages,' Caitlin called over as I approached.

'I showed Sam Maes Camlan,' I explained as I sat down by the fire pit and warmed my hands. 'He really loves all the Arthurian history.'

'Takes after you then, Dad,' she said as she held up a can of bitter. 'Drink?'

'Why not?' I said, aware that a car was coming up the track. Despite what I now knew about TJ and Dean Ashcroft, I was still wary and on my guard.

Caitlin frowned. 'Expecting anyone?'

'No, I'm not.' I shook my head as I walked over to the track to see who was coming. I glanced towards the stables and could see Sam closing up the doors.

'You okay, mate?' I shouted.

He nodded and gave me a wave.

I could feel myself tensing as I watched the approaching vehicle. Then I gave a little whistle and watched as Jack, who had been dozing by the fire pit, came bounding over to my side.

'Good boy,' I said, scruffing the top of his head and watching the track like a hawk. There wasn't time for me to pop in and grab my shotgun before the vehicle arrived.

The stillness was broken by the sudden hoot of an owl from a tree in the nearby woods.

A black Astra appeared from round the corner.

Phew.

With a sense of relief, I saw that it was Kelly driving.

I gave her a little wave.

She pulled over, parked up, and got out.

'Hi Kelly,' I said brightly as Jack and I wandered over to greet her.

'Hi Frank,' she said with a smile. She lifted up a bottle of Jameson's. 'I brought you a present.'

'You didn't need to do that,' I said. 'Jameson's?'

'I asked around the station and that's what everyone told me you drank.' She shook her head. 'It seems very inadequate given that you saved my life but it's all I could think of.'

I glanced down at Jack. 'Technically, it was Jack who actually knocked Ian flying.'

Kelly smiled. 'Oh right. Well, I'll bring something for him next time.'

'Any news on Judy Thompson?' I asked.

'Out of danger and should make a full recovery,' she replied. 'I've no idea if she'll pursue anything against the police though. And Ian ... Stuart Jones ... is on remand awaiting trial.'

I sighed. 'He pleaded 'not guilty'?'

'I'm afraid so.'

'What a prick.'

'Apparently he bought a fake birth certificate about ten years ago and created a whole new identity. How that wasn't spotted when he joined the force, God only knows.'

I gave her an understanding look and then gestured over to the firepit. 'Why don't you come over and have a drink with us?'

She hesitated. 'No, it's okay. I don't want to intrude.'

'Don't be daft. I won't take no for an answer.'

'Okay then. You've twisted my arm.' She laughed and

then stared at me, deep wrinkles forming on her brow. 'Thank you, Frank. I wouldn't be standing here if it wasn't for you.'

I shrugged. 'No problem. Come on. We've got some wine in the fridge.'

Chapter 51

Opening my eyes slowly, I realised that the telly was still on. I glanced over and saw that Rachel was asleep in her armchair. Jack was circling by the door and making a whining noise which must have woken me up. I got up slowly with a slight groan. I assumed that he was whining because he wanted to go out.

'That's okay, boy,' I reassured him.

Then he pawed and scratched at the door frantically.

That's strange.

Something was wrong.

I opened the door to the hallway and walked towards the front door. 'What is it?' I asked him.

He barked a couple of times.

I was starting to feel uneasy.

As I opened the front door cautiously, I suddenly saw what was making Jack so unsettled.

The stable was on fire.

Jesus Christ!

Breaking into a sprint, I ran full pelt down the path.

From what I could see, the far wall and some of the stable's roof was engulfed in flames.

How the hell has that happened?

Grabbing the huge wooden doors, I threw them open and was hit by a wall of heat and smoke.

I coughed and squinted.

Duke and Lleuad were whinnying loudly, their hooves clattering as they kicked the wooden sides of the stable in terror.

The heat from the fire was intense.

I pulled off my t-shirt and wrapped it around my nose and mouth.

Jogging in, I peered through the thick smoke.

Pulling back the bolt, I managed to get one of the split doors open.

As I went to grab Duke, he reared up and I ducked to avoid his flailing hooves.

'Come on, boy. It's okay, come on.' I tried to reassure him as I pulled him out and guided him quickly outside.

My eyes were stinging and raw from the smoke.

I coughed, trying to clear my lungs.

Taking a deep breath of air, I ran back into the stable again to get Lleuad.

The rafters above me were now engulfed in fierce orange flames.

Getting to where Lleuad was kicking and whinnying, I managed to open the split door.

'Come on, boy,' I shouted over the noise of the fire. 'Come on.'

I tried to guide him out, but he was so scared that he just kicked out at me.

I glanced up, and saw that the beams above us were starting to split. It was only a matter of time before the whole roof collapsed.

'Come on, Lleuad,' I urged him as I encouraged him out.

I heard the cracking sound of splitting wood.

'Come on!' I shouted.

He turned, barged past me, and cantered out to where Duke was waiting.

Thank God.

They were both safe.

I approached the two horses, preparing to get them into the safety of the paddock.

Suddenly, I saw headlights on the track.

What the hell is going on?

Then I heard the sound of a shotgun.

CRACK!

Breaking into a sprint, I saw a white transit van parked outside the annexe.

It was the same van I'd seen over in the woods.

'Shit!'

My heart was thundering and my eyes raw and watery from the smoke.

What's going on?

The van suddenly pulled away with a screech of its tyres and headed down the track and away from where I was running.

Someone was standing on the path of the annexe.

It was Caitlin.

She was holding a shotgun.

'Caitlin?' I yelled in panic.

'He's got Sam!' she screamed. 'TJ has got Sam!'

Then I noticed a body lying on the ground nearby.

It was Dean Ashgrove. He had a huge gunshot wound to his chest.

'Dad!' Caitlin wailed.

'I'm going after them,' I yelled as I ran off towards my truck. 'Call the police and fire brigade.'

As I reached my truck, I saw to my despair that they'd stabbed all four tyres.

I sprinted back towards Caitlin's car but they'd done the same to her tyres too.

I FELT sick as I stopped and looked around.

In the distance, the rear lights of the van slowly disappeared.

At that moment, my whole world shattered into a thousand pieces.

What am I going to do?

Enjoy This Book?
PREORDER THE NEXT FRANK MARSHAL BOOK NOW

My Book
https://www.amazon.com/dp/B0F638T4QM

Five Days In Provence
27TH JUNE 2025

HERE ARE THE FIRST TWO CHAPTERS OF MY NEW PSYCHOLOGICAL THRILLER

1 August 2022

A shadowy figure emerges slowly from a bank of acrid smoke. It looks otherworldly. Ethereal. I can't see who it is yet.

I cough as the smoke catches on my throat. My eyes are stinging and raw. I don't care.

We have to find her.

What the hell happened? How could she just vanish? I ask myself. Nothing feels real.

I rub my eyes, blink frantically and look around.

The view from halfway up Mont Ventoux is completely obscured by a thick carpet of smoke from the wildfires below us. As the noisy wind picks up, it blows the smoke into frightening, circular twists like a mini hurricane. The horizon has all but disappeared.

This is all my fault. It was my idea. My trip. My fiftieth birthday we were all celebrating.

The figure is now only ten yards away. I can see it's Shaun, the Irishman who is renovating the farmhouse opposite from where we are staying. He and Tom, the guy working with him, had been out cycling when I rang them for help.

'What is it?' I ask anxiously.

'Tom's found her,' he replies.

My whole body reacts with relief.

But then I can see that there's something wrong. He has a grim expression on his face.

Why does he look so serious? It's good that they've found her, isn't it?

'Is she all right?' I ask nervously.

Shaun gestures to the ridge. 'Tom's trying to get down to her now,' he explains sounding a little flustered.

'Show me,' I say, my pulse racing.

I follow Shaun through the smoke, waving my hands in front of my face as if this would somehow disperse it.

'Have you seen the others?' he asks.

'Not yet.' I point to our right. 'I assume they're still up the other path.'

Another figure appears, coming towards us. It's Tom.

The smoke catches on my throat again. I start to cough.

As Tom reaches us, he pulls off his rucksack, takes a large steel water bottle from a side pocket and hands it to me. 'Here you go, Steph.'

'Thanks,' I splutter as I take a few sips which seem to clear my throat. 'Can you see her?'

Tom nods but he wears the same sombre expression as Shaun. 'She's about fifty yards down the slope. But it's really steep.'

I spot another furtive glance between Tom and Shaun.

'What?' I ask in a curt but anxious tone. 'What is it?'

Shaun looks at me. 'From the way she's lying…' He stops.

1 August 2022

I frown with a growing sense of dread deep in the pit of my stomach. 'What?'

'I think… she might be dead.'

31 July 2022

'Where's that fucking wine?' Darcie checks her watch again. Ten minutes since she'd asked the flight attendant to bring more white wine. Her fingers drum against the armrest, fighting the urge to press the call button. The diazepam she'd taken before boarding isn't quite cutting through her flight anxiety, and she needs something stronger than travel-sized wine to dull the edge.

'You're not in business class now, you snob,' Abi laughs.

Darcie starts to unbuckle her seatbelt. I'll go and get it myself then, she thinks.

'Where are you going?' Abi says with a quizzical frown.

Darcie shrugs. 'If Mohammed won't come to the mountain.'

Abi rolls her eyes. 'It's "If the mountain won't come to Mohammed…"'

'Is it? Well, whatever.' Darcie sighs. 'Who was Mohammed?'

'No idea.'

Darcie sees the spindly young steward Wayne coming

31 July 2022

down the aisle of their budget aeroplane with four miniature bottles of white wine and a card machine.

'Ah, about time,' she mutters under her breath.

'Here we go,' Wayne says, placing down the bottles on their grey, plastic fold-out trays. He starts to tap at the card machine.

'I thought you'd forgotten all about us,' Darcie says in a spiky tone. How long does it take to retrieve four tiny bottles and ferry them back, for God's sake? I could train a monkey to do that.

'Oh, right. Sorry,' Wayne says, looking embarrassed.

Darcie feels Abi giving her a sharp nudge with her elbow.

'You've forgotten my ice.' Darcie sighs again. The only way to drink the horrible, cheap plonk that they served on this substandard airline was to put ice in it and get it to a temperature where she couldn't really taste it.

Wayne pulls an apologetic face. 'Have I?'

'Yes,' Darcie replies in a tone that leaves him in no doubt that she isn't impressed.

She doesn't care. That was his job.

'I'm sorry.' Wayne seems flustered. 'This machine is playing up today.'

'Don't worry at all.' Abi jumps in with a warm smile, touching his arm. 'Wi-Fi is always terrible on flights. And you've been run off your feet.'

Darcie rolls her eyes. Classic Abi – always smoothing things over, just like she had when they were eleven years old at Milton Hall and Darcie had reduced a supply teacher to tears. Some things never change.

'Not your fault,' Abi reassures him.

'Right, got it.' Wayne sighs with relief.

Darcie slides her business debit card across the tray with a practised flick. The shiny black Amex with 'Darcie

Miller Media' embossed in silver. Her accountant's voice echoes in her head: *Just run everything through the business, darling. First class, Champagne, the lot. I'll sort out what's kosher later.* The same delicious thrill she gets every time she signs off an 'influencer lunch' or 'content research trip' – that little dance on the edge of what's legal. Like shoplifting expensive lipsticks as a teenager, but now with better clothes and a better alibi.

'There we go,' Wayne says politely as he hands Darcie her card. Then he turns and walks back down towards the front of the plane.

'Christ, he was exceptionally inept, wasn't he?' Darcie says in her best withering tone.

'Oh, Darcie, does it really matter?' Same old Abi, still trying to smooth her friend's sharp edges after all these years.

'Yes, it bloody well does. And bollocks to you,' Darcie cackles. 'Cheers.'

'Santé,' Abi says as they click their 'glasses' together.

'This plastic has such a lovely ring to it, doesn't it?' Darcie snorts caustically. She then takes a long glug of wine.

That's better.

'Such a snob.' Abi's eye-roll holds nearly forty years of affectionate exasperation.

Darcie grins. She plays up to be that way just for the effect. 'That's why you love me.'

Abi points over at Steph. 'Last of us to turn fifty.' Then she gives Darcie a sarcastic smile. 'You didn't even celebrate your fiftieth. We went for that little dinner and you banned us from posting any photos.'

'That's because I'm actually in my mid to late forties.' Darcie forces a smile.

'Remember?'

31 July 2022

'All about your brand, is it?' Abi says knowingly.

'I can't have the yummy mummies of metropolitan London thinking that I'm in my fifties now. That would never do.'

'No, God forbid,' Abi snorts.

They fall into silence as they drink.

Darcie then leans in and whispers the burning secret that has been on her lips for the past two hours. 'I slept with someone else.'

Abi's eyes widen as she splutters into her wine. 'You slept with someone else again? Jesus!' she exclaims. 'I thought you were going to stop shagging random people.'

Darcie has been married to Hugo for over twenty years.

'Shsh.' Darcie puts her finger to her lips. 'Say it a bit louder, I don't think the pilot heard.'

'When?'

'About a month ago. We spent a few nights together, actually.'

'That's not like you, is it?'

'No.' Darcie shrugs. 'It felt different this time.'

'Really?'

Darcie nods. 'Really.'

The tension in her body evaporates now she's told her oldest, best friend. It might be childish, but she also gets a frisson of excitement at sharing the secret and Abi's reaction.

Abi looks at her in disbelief. 'Who the hell was it?' she asks as her voice drops to a whisper.

Darcie nods with a smirk.

'Come on,' Darcie says. 'You can't be that surprised. I've told you about me and Hugo. The last three years have been particularly horrible since he started drinking too much. What am I meant to do?'

31 July 2022

'Why don't you just leave him?' Abi suggests – not for the first time.

'I don't know,' Darcie groans. 'I know I should.' What she doesn't like to admit, especially to herself, is that she and Hugo are a brand. She gets invited to film premieres and parties because she's married to Hugo, even if his star is on the wane. If they divorce, she can no longer play at 'happy families' and being a celebrity couple for her online fans. It's not a risk she wants to take after all the hard work she's put in over the years.

'I saw him on that panel show last week,' Abi says carefully. 'He seemed...'

'Drunk? Slurring his words?' Darcie gives a bitter laugh. 'The producers had to edit around him. His agent has suggested a stint in rehab. He just sits there every night drowning his sorrows, full of self-pity, banging on about that BAFTA he won twenty years ago and how no one's offering him proper acting roles anymore.' She takes a long swig of wine. 'You know what he said when that psycho broke into our house and held a knife to my throat? Nothing. Because he was passed out on the sofa with an empty bottle of Scotch. Thank God Bella's away at uni and doesn't have to watch her father destroy himself.'

There are a few seconds of silence. Abi finishes her wine and then looks at Darcie.

'I knew you'd had a few one-night stands recently,' Abi says, wide-eyed, in a hushed voice. 'But another affair, Darcie? I thought you said never again.'

'It's not an affair.' Darcie gives her a shrug. 'But Hugo and I haven't shagged for three years, Abs. What am I meant to do, not have sex from now until the day I die? And I don't want to have to pay for it. But I do love sex.'

A woman in her sixties who's sitting in the row in front

of them turns around as Darcie says the last phrase a little too loudly.

'Oh, hello?' Darcie says to the woman in a sarcastically chirpy tone that's intended to suggest *Turn the fuck around and mind your own business.*

Abi gives her another dig in the ribs. 'Darcie.'

'Oops,' Darcie sniggers.

'Who is he?' Abi asks.

Darcie isn't about to divulge this information. Well, not yet.

'I can't tell you,' she admits.

'What? You tell me everything,' Abi protests.

Darcie shakes her head and mimes zipping her lips shut. 'I can't.'

Abi frowns. 'Bloody hell! You can't tell me that you're having an affair with someone and then not tell me who it's with.'

'I can't tell you.' Darcie pulls a face. 'But it's a bit of a shocker, to be honest.'

'You mean I know him?' Abi asks.

'Yes. I'll probably crack and tell you when I'm shit-faced in the next few days.' Darcie sighs. 'And don't tell the others.'

The air steward Wayne appears at Darcie's side, smiles and hands her a plastic beaker with ice cubes inside. 'There you go.'

'Thanks,' Darcie says.

Abi gives her a pressing look. 'Darcie, you cow! Tell me!'

Darcie undoes her seatbelt, hands Abi her glass, pushes up the tray and stands up.

'Hold that. I'm going for a pee.'

31 July 2022

Steph's birthday celebration is about to take a dark turn… Be the first to read Five Days in Provence.

https://geni.us/927-al-aut-am

Your FREE book is waiting for you now

Get your FREE copy of the prequel to
the DI Ruth Hunter Series NOW
http://www.simonmccleave.com/vip-email-club
and join my VIP Email Club

DC RUTH HUNTER SERIES

London, 1997. A series of baffling murders. A web of political corruption. DC Ruth Hunter thinks she has the brutal killer in her sights, but there's one problem. He's a Serbian war criminal who died five years earlier and lies buried in Bosnia.

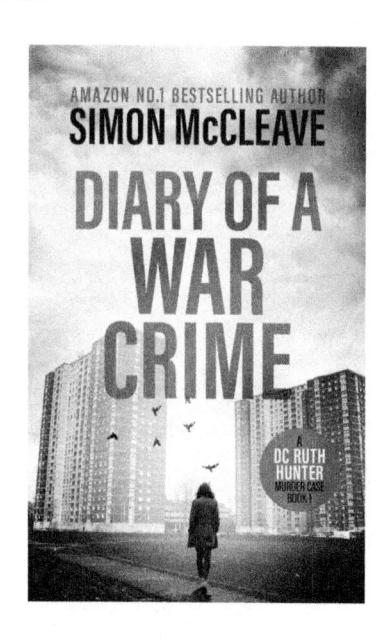

My Book
My Book

AUTHOR'S NOTE

Although this book is very much a work of fiction, it is located in Snowdonia, a spectacular area of North Wales. It is steeped in history and folklore that spans over two thousand years. I have made liberal use of artistic licence, names and places have been changed to enhance the pace and substance of the story.

Acknowledgments

I will always be indebted to the people who have made this novel possible.

My mum, Pam, and my stronger half, Nicola, whose initial reaction, ideas and notes on my work I trust implicitly. Keira, for her patience and hard work. Carole Kendal for her meticulous proofreading. My designer Stuart Bache for yet another incredible cover design. My superb agent, Millie Hoskins at United Agents, and Dave Gaughran for his invaluable support and advice.

Printed in Great Britain
by Amazon